AS MEAN AS THE NIGHT

A collection by Rick McQuiston

All stories copyright 1999-2008

All rights reserved.

Edited by Rick and Rosemary McQuiston.

All stories, characters, and events are fictional and the product of the author's imagination.

Cover concept and artwork by Rick McQuiston, Rick McQuiston Jr.

Technical support from Amanda McQuiston, Walonda McQuiston, and Rick Valle.

Email: Many_Midnights@yahoo.com

Website: many-midnights.webs.com

ISBN# 978-1-105-69227-7

Welcome.

I proudly offer here for your reading pleasure 15 more tales of terror. Each and every one of these little fear-inducers was handpicked by myself.

Admittingly, it was difficult narrowing them down to only 15, but I stuck with it and managed to churn these up from the very depths of darkness with only the flickering light from a blood-red candle to guide me.

There are stories about nightmares, alien invasions, demons, and even one about Christmas, which I simply had to include due to its creepiness.

So please, light a candle (blood-red of course), pour a hot cauldron of tea and delve into my tales, where the night is much, much meaner than the day.

CONTENTS

THE THING IN THE BACKYARD	1
ANDY'S LAMP	7
THE ROPE	11
THE INSTINCT TO SURVIVE	17
CHANGES IN APPETITE	23
BELIEVE	25
THE SPEED DEMON	29
IN THE DARK	35
FLOWER IN THE WIND	43
MEMORIES OF INHUMAN NATURE	53
WHAT TANGLED WEBS WE WEAVE	61
A NIGHTMARE YOU DON'T WANT TO TEMPT	67
THINGS HAVE A WAY OF COMING BACK AROUND	71
CHRISTMAS MORNING	79
AS MEAN AS THE NIGHT	83

THE THING IN THE BACKYARD

Ronnie felt the cool damp grass beneath his feet as he stood in the middle of his backyard, looking around for any signs of danger. He wasn't exactly sure how he wound up there. The last thing he remembered he was sleeping comfortably in his bed, reviewing Jenny Simone's beautiful smile in his mind.

Overhead, a thick layer of clouds quickly moved in, blotting out the full moon and leaving Ronnie standing in near total darkness. The backyard held him in the palm of its hand, subject to its desires, its dangers.

"Hello? Is anyone there?" Ronnie called out, fully aware that he was all alone. "Is there anybody there?"

And then something in the darkness shifted; something big and very near to where he stood.

Ronnie was unable to move. He sensed where his house was, but somehow he knew if he turned around it wouldn't be there anymore. Its location was controlled by the backyard.

The noises were getting closer, and Ronnie started panicking. He knew he couldn't stay where he was. His only option was to run for it.

As soon as he took his first step the thing in the darkness groaned in rage. It was following him, smashing into trees as it went. Ronnie also heard other noises as well. Noises that sounded like whatever was following him was ripping pieces from itself and hurling them in all directions. Loud, wet thuds filled Ronnie's ears when the thing's parts crashed into trees or splattered on the ground. It sounded like rotten melons hitting a hot sidewalk.

Ronnie stumbled through the darkness, well aware that whatever was behind him was gaining. His house was nowhere to be found, despite him feeling the hard, cracked concrete of his back patio. He accidentally bumped into his dad's barbeque, which crashed to the ground. His dad would be so mad at him if he found out. The barbeque was brand new, only a week old. A smile crept on Ronnie's face when he recalled how excited his dad was about the upcoming barbeque season. But now his dad wouldn't have a grill to cook on.

    Regaining his footing, Ronnie whirled around and was forced to stop dead in his tracks. A sixth sense told him there was a crater in front of him. To move forward would surely cause him to fall into it. Only empty black space greeted his eyes, space that was not willing to reveal what it hid.

    And then Ronnie remembered that his dad always kept a flashlight in the yard, usually hanging near the barbeque. He reached out into the darkness and with great relief latched onto the flashlight. The fact that it wasn't attached to anything was not lost on him, but the impossibility of a flashlight dangling in midair simply wasn't his first concern at the moment. He flicked it on and swung the light to where his house should have been. And just as he suspected, there was nothing there.

    The thin beam of light from the flashlight trailed off into the vast sea of black, revealing absolutely nothing except a cold, empty void, which seemed to slide into an endlessly deep chasm.

    Ronnie heard the things scampering around in the dark behind him. There were dozens of them scuttling back and forth, hissing and fighting with each other, trying to get into the right position for their assault. However, the large thing which had been chasing him had stopped its pursuit. It shifted from side to side but did not attack. Ronnie wanted to flash the light on it but his fear stopped him. After all, did he really want to see it?

    But on the other hand, knowing what he was facing could help him to escape. Without a second thought he splashed the light on the creature, on the thing in the backyard.

    A tall, painfully-thin man glared back at Ronnie. His eyes were bright red and his complexion chalk-white. He reminded Ronnie of a vampire. He smiled a chilling smile, which allowed Ronnie to see the hundreds of tiny, needle-like teeth in his oversized mouth, each and every one curved and jagged as a fat green tongue rolled around between them. Ronnie also noticed one more thing before his flashlight went out…the man was busy pulling pieces of himself off and flinging them in all directions. The gaping holes in his body were then immediately filled back in as if nothing had happened.

"Eventually one will stick," the deep, thick voice growled. "One will manage to break through. Doors will open. You'll see boy. You'll see."

Frantically trying to get his flashlight to work again, Ronnie shook it vigorously, but it still didn't work.

"You'll see boy," the horrible voice teased from the darkness. "You'll see."

Ronnie felt a wave of relief wash over him when the flashlight finally kicked on. He immediately scanned the rest of the yard hoping to find an alternate escape route.

But all he saw were the worms.

Or at least things which looked like worms. There were dozens of them slithering in all directions like blind rats searching for food. Their soulless eyes gleamed brightly when the light flashed on them, and the hissing sound they made was almost too much to bear. Some seemed to be trying to scratch their way into the ground and the trees. Glistening claws on their undersides gyrated up and down in frenzied blurs, almost too fast to even see.

And then the terrible voice spoke again.

"Here boy, catch."

Ronnie whirled around just in time to see the tall, pale man tear off his own head and hurl it high into the night air. The horrible thing landed with a sick thud at Ronnie's feet and glared up at him with an evil smile. Sharp claws sprouted from its sides as it began to emit a high-pitched hiss. It was starting to dig into the ground just like the worm things were doing. Ronnie avoided shining the light on the man;
he knew he'd already have a new head by then and didn't want to see it. Without thinking he turned and ran toward where his house had been, hoping he wouldn't fall into a bottomless pit.

And then the wail of his alarm clock woke him up.

Had it all been a dream? Ronnie could only hope so. The mere thought of the tall, pale man tossing pieces of his body across the backyard made him feel sick to his stomach.

But what about the Tall Man's words?

One will stick. Doors will open.

What the heck did they mean?

Forcing himself to leave the comfort of his bed Ronnie walked over to the window and looked into the backyard. It was a beautiful morning, clear and warm, accented with a gentle breeze from the north. He watched several small birds fly by overhead and a pair of black squirrels scamper up a nearby tree. All appeared normal and peaceful. Satisfied, he closed the window and crawled back into bed, intent on another hour or two of sleep.

The uneasy feeling that he was being watched nagged Ronnie in his sleep. He sat up in bed and looked around his room, but nothing appeared out of place. But then something caught his attention.

A shadow about the size of a basketball dangled outside his window, swaying back and forth in the wind. Ronnie couldn't see it too clearly; it was partially obscured by the sun's glare. His heart skipped a beat when two red eyes opened on it and focused on him in bed.

It was the Tall Man's head!

Its eyes stared at Ronnie as a greasy smile slid across its face, revealing jagged teeth and a thick green tongue. Beneath it, sharp claws scratched furiously, as if trying to dig into the air itself.

Fighting the urge to throw up, Ronnie slid out of bed and picked up his baseball bat. He gripped it tightly and took a cautious step towards the window. The thing was still smiling at him, its tongue now hanging out of its mouth, as it hissed quietly through the glass. It knew something. Something that Ronnie didn't.

Heavy wet thuds from the hallway echoed in the bedroom. Ronnie knew very well what they were. The Tall Man was busy tossing parts of his body around again. Ronnie noticed the slimy footprints on his floor then. And he also noticed his bedroom door cracked open, even though he had closed it before he went to bed.

The guilt of having unleashed something terrible on the world weighed heavily on his mind. And then another even more disturbing thought occurred to him. What if there were other tall, pale men out there who were only waiting for something to stick?

ANDY'S LAMP

The lamp had moved, Andy was sure of it. The soft yellow glow from the 60-watt bulb had shifted slightly, causing vague shadows in the room to move as if alive. Granted it wasn't much movement, but it was there. There was no doubt about it.

Andy forced himself to relax, settling back into his worn recliner with his small caliber semi-automatic handgun resting in his lap. It was an older model, a gift from his senile grandfather, but it still worked effectively. The silencer he bought for it had proved to be money well spent. Silence was a necessity in his situation. He couldn't afford to let any of his neighbors hear anything out of the ordinary, such as a gun firing.

He focused on the lamp again, studying it closely, waiting for it to move again. It wore its pale yellow shade like a hat. Fondling the trigger of the gun he swore to himself that he would take action this time if anything moved. This time he wouldn't hesitate. This time he would be ready.

Several minutes elapsed. The monotonous ticking of the wall clock was the only sound in the house, echoing in the room. Andy was fighting sleep, his weary mind drifting in and out of consciousness. He knew very well that falling asleep could be a big mistake, but still found himself dozing off. The last time he did the spider thing came, slithering out of the refrigerator, week old milk and cheese dripping from its bloated body. He had woken up just in time to flatten it with a few sharp swings from his trusty baseball bat, *Woody*.

Eventually he had abandoned his bat in favor of a more versatile and efficient weapon, his gun. In a strange way he actually was anxious for the spider thing to appear again. Surely bullets would do a far more effective job of dispatching it than good old Woody.

His troubled mind wandered back to the first time the spider thing had appeared. He had just come home from work, back when he had a job, and promptly fastened himself to his chair in front of the television set. He was tired and suffering from a cold and all he wanted to do was flip through channels, a routine that he found himself slipping into more and more frequently. As the newscast lady read about the day's events her pretty face started to distort. Her light blue eyes slid apart further and further until they were next to her ears. And from the vacant spaces where they had been emerged the glowing evil of the spider thing, its thick skull splitting open the lady's head as it snaked its way into the light of the news station room.

    Next came the legs, which sprouted from the sides of the TV and immediately began to thrash up and down as if throwing a fit. The appendages were thin, almost skeletal, and were covered in glistening slime.

    The newscast lady continued on about a horrible car accident that morning on Interstate 696, completely oblivious to the swollen abdomen rising directly behind her head. She was pretty still, although in a horror movie type of way now, and Andy found himself wondering if he was hallucinating.

    But he wasn't.

    The spider thing's razor sharp fangs clicked together methodically, dripping a foul greenish substance that Andy guessed was some type of venom. It focused its multiple eyes on Andy then, and he before he knew what he was doing he ran to his bedroom and grabbed old Woody and ended the nightmare, and his TV, with three quick swings.

    There it was again! The lamp had moved! Andy raised his gun slightly, leveling it at the inanimate object as he pondered whether or not to finally take action. The lamp stood motionless on the end table, illuminating the room with its yellowed light. It almost dared him to fire at it. He watched it methodically, still undecided if he should blow the thing apart before it changed, before the spider thing came. Too many times in the past he had waited too long.

    One time the spider thing nearly got to him, grazing its jagged teeth along his forearm, leaving a four-inch scar and undeniable proof of its existence. Since then if he ever doubted that it was all real all he needed to do was to look at his arm.

The lamp started to jiggle, a little at first, but then much more pronounced. It jerked forward, then backwards. Its lampshade shifted to one side. The light bulb shattered. The cord slipped out of the wall socket and swung high into the air before crashing down to the floor. Andy watched in horror as the glistening legs slid out from the sides of the lamp. For all the mental preparation he had done he still found himself shaking considerably, so much so that he had trouble steadying his gun on the creature.

The face of the spider thing emerged from the lamp and focused on Andy, hissing at him so loudly that a small mirror on a nearby wall cracked. Andy stared into the dull, emotionless eyes of the thing. He saw his distorted reflection in its eyes. He saw his death.

Gathering what strength he could Andy leveled his gun at the thing's head. He squeezed the trigger four times in quick succession, each rattling his already frail nerves. And after the smoke cleared he leaned forward to view his handiwork.

All he saw was a shattered lamp. Sharp pieces of it lay strewn all across the table and floor and four bullet holes decorated the wall. Andy grunted in disgust. The mess was terrible and would require a lot of cleanup.

How could he have missed it? Where was its body? And why no blood?

There was however another explanation.

Perhaps it was all in his mind. Hallucinations. Stress. Imagination. Maybe he had just imagined the whole thing.

But what about the wound on his arm? Surely that was proof the thing existed.

But then he remembered the accident he had when he was fixing his truck. A sudden slip with a large screwdriver and bingo…a huge, bloody gash. Just like the one on his arm.

Feeling relieved for the first time in days Andy suddenly realized he was hungry. Sauntering into the kitchen he made himself a quick sandwich. Disturbing thoughts interrupted his meal though, such as where the thing had come from in the first place or what it really wanted. But there was nothing he could do about it now. One way or another it was gone.

    He finished his meal and fell back into his recliner half asleep. For the first time in ages he was able to completely relax, finally not having to worry about being attacked by alien spider monsters. He would work on bettering himself. First thing in the morning he would scan the want ads for any available job he could lay his hands on. And then he would ask the cute girl across the street out on a date. And then he would look for a nicer car.

    He found himself periodically looking over at the remains of his lamp, just to make sure there wasn't anything attempting to crawl out of it, but saw nothing except for splintered pieces of it lying on the floor.

    Eventually he started to doze off. The day had been a long one and he was very tired. So tired that he didn't notice the thin legs sliding out from one of the shattered pieces of the lamp.

THE ROPE

The woods surrounded Chris at every turn. Trees with barren, dry branches arched in from all directions like tentacles groping for nourishment. Occasionally one would scrape his face or brush against his orange vest, but he paid them no attention. After all, hunting had certain aspects one had to endure. The cold was one. Eighteen degrees, wind chill five. But the thermal underwear and socks Kathy bought him last Christmas handled those problems. The loneliness was another problem. Even though he had come up this year with Terry and Frank, they had decided to go their own ways to increase their chances of spotting a buck and decrease their visibility. But no one to talk to seemed to dampen the fun of the trip. It did, however, net Chris an eight-pointer last season, and for that, he'd endure these solitary times.

This season was quiet a different story though. The noticeable absence of deer, or any other animal for that matter, puzzled as well as frustrated him. Two days out here, and hardly a single animal. No deer, no rabbits, hell, not even a squirrel. He felt his mind wandering to compensate for the lack of action. He thought of Kathy and how she was bugging him to have a kid. He would love having a kid, preferably a boy so he could take him out hunting when he was old enough, but he had always been afraid. He has seen videos of birth. Messy situation. He confided to himself that he didn't want Kathy to go through that, or at least not yet.

Besides, he was only 33 and Kathy was 29. Surly there was plenty of time for kids. The wind was picking up now, bringing with it a nasty chill. He buttoned his vest and slipped his cap on and continued onward. Dry, brittle leaves crushed underfoot as the wind slammed against his face, searching for any exposed areas. Frustration started to swell to anger. This is bullshit, he thought. Three hundred dollars on a new gun, a hundred on a new suit and two hundred and fifty miles of driving, for what! To walk around in these God forsaken woods for two days. He started to head back to his truck. But then he became suddenly aware that he was lost. Nothing looked familiar. Feeling a bit panicky, he did that only thing he could do… he trudged on.

Then he thought of something. He wondered if he was heading for Osanka Country. Three years earlier, a couple of hunters had disappeared there. Three experienced hunters. No trace was ever found of them except their guns and one of their hats. Chris had heard the stories from Frank. His wife worked with the men's wives. Frank also told him that besides the guns and hat the Rangers had found a peculiar rope coming out of the ground. One of them tried to dig it out, but gave up after going down a couple of feet. Frank had said that the rope was a big one too, a couple of inches thick with a sort of sticky residue on it.

Chris soon found himself scanning the ground for the rope. He wanted to see if he was in the area of the disappearances.

But what the heck did it attach to? And did it have any connection with the men vanishing?

These questions swirled in Chris's mind, causing him to develop a small migraine. Stress always did this to him, and this was about as stressed as he had ever been.

Hours passed. It was now past four o'clock. It would be getting dark soon and he was still lost. He had to be near Osanka County. He knew he was heading north and that would lead him through Osanka.

But his food and water were starting to run low and his ankle was bothering him.

Stupid molehill, he thought angrily, remembering his mishap while cutting the grass. Should've had checked to make sure it was healing properly. Now it was going to cause him trouble. How could he possibly trudge though miles of woods on a bad ankle? No one to blame but himself though. God how he hated it when he did stupid crap like this. But what's done is done. No use crying over spilt milk, especially when you were the one who knocked the glass over.

Glancing at his watch, he groaned. Four forty-three. Still no sight of anything. Plus as an added bonus, his back was getting sore from his equipment. Always packed too much stuff for these trips. Soon, he'd have to lighten his load. Three hundred bucks for his new fifty caliber Knight T-bolt rifle. And to think that he'd have to just leave it on the ground for some lucky schmuck to stumble on it. Now he really had a headache.

45 minutes later, he spotted the first living thing he'd seen in nearly two days: a fellow hunter, his bright orange vest moving silently in search of deer.

Although the man was roughly 200 yards away, Chris started yelling as loud as he could.

"Help! I'm injured. Help!" His ankle throbbed and thirst gripped his throat but he had to get this man's attention.

Finally the man reacted. Turning toward Chris, he raised his gun in a fellow hunter's salute. Apparently though, he failed to notice Chris's situation or condition. He would have to go to him. Moving forward however, was now more difficult than ever. His ankle had swollen to where his boot was actually becoming a hindrance. Ten feet felt like a mile. The man, now seeing Chris stumbling toward him, started to run as well, although it looked like he was running away from something.

Feeling himself lose his balance, courtesy of a grapefruit-sized rock, Chris fell forward. His hands met with dry leaves and twigs while dirt peppered his face, leaving him with a bad taste in his mouth.

He blacked out.

When he came to, Chris felt even more disoriented. His watch revealed that he had been out only ten minutes, but his head ached with a pain equal to his ankle. Looking up, he could see no trace of the man who had been running toward him only moments before.

"I can't believe this," he thought out loud. "What's next? A snow storm!"

Despite his condition, he gingerly stood up and brushed off his clothes, doing his best to ignore his injuries.

"Hello? Is anybody out there?" His words met silence. Only the wind careening trough the trees could be heard.

Slowly, painfully, he started to limp in the direction of where the man had been. He withdrew his blade. The six-inch Buck knife felt good in his hand. Since leaving his rifle behind, it was the first time he felt safe.

"Hello…Hello? I need help; I'm lost and injured. Hello?"

Within a few minutes, he reached the area where the man had been. It was obvious that something happened there. Leaves and twigs were scattered around as if there had been a scuffle of some sort, but the man was nowhere to be found.

And then Chris noticed the rope.

Approximately ten feet in length, it snaked inconspicuously through the leaves. Fear paralyzed his mind. He was in the same spot where those men had disappeared three years earlier! And worse still was that now another man had disappeared, and practically right before him? Turning slowly, he gripped his knife with a renewed zeal. But he felt a new sensation start to manifest itself within him…curiosity.

As he approached the rope, Chris's ankle reminded him of his condition. A quick makeshift bandage from the inside coat pocket lessened the discomfort. Now he could take a closer look at the rope.

It appeared no different than any other heavy-gauge hemp rope other than it had a sticky residue covering it. Deciding that self-preservation overrules curiosity, Chris backed away from the rope.

Three steps back, he stumbled on something, causing him to crash to the ground. A small lump under the leaves caught his eye. Horror strangled his mind as the bloody cap, which partly concealed a mutilated hand, came into view. He could still see the band on the ring finger.

The rope was outstretched before him as if hiding a terrible secret. He stared at it.

Where could it lead to?

Brushing the dirt from his vest, he started to walk away. After three or four steps, he heard a sound that under any other situation would be nothing out of the ordinary.

But not now. Not here. Not with the rope the only thing behind him. The sound of leaves gently rustling froze his legs in their tracks. He slowly turned to meet an impossible sight.

The rope was slithering its way through the leaves toward him. Moving similar to a snake, it somehow sensed where he was. It coiled up as if to strike, much the same way a snake would. No teeth or mouth on the thing allowed Chris to dispel some of his fear and ready himself for a fight. Shear adrenaline rejuvenated his ankle enough for him to firmly plant himself in a fighting stance.

"Come on! Let's go! I'll cut ya down a couple of yards and use you in my truck!"

The rope started to dance in the air. It abruptly hung a sharp left, darting toward Chris`s left foot.

Regaining his balance, Chris now took to the offensive. He leaned inward, trying to distract it with his empty hand. But the rope reacted as if it had eyes. It methodically followed his hand like a dog to a biscuit. Seizing the opportunity, he swung his knife in a deadly arc. The blade kissed the rope as a ten-inch length was served cleanly from its end.

"Take that!" he screamed.

But his victory was short-lived though as the rope recoiled itself and released a new onslaught. It now raised itself almost straight up, towering over its now puny opponent.

Chris knew he had to abandon the fight. If he could just get fifteen or twenty feet away, it wouldn't be able to reach him then.

The rope hovered silently, seemingly oblivious to its prey retreating. Chris continued to slowly move backward, ignoring his throbbing ankle. Each step moved him closer to safety. When he was far enough away, he would simply turn and run.

As he prepared himself to make his escape, he felt heat from where the rope met the ground.

There, at the base of the rope, the ground was opening up. Although opening up would have been a wrong description to use. *Melting* would have been more appropriate. The leaves; the twigs; the dirt; it was all dissolving into the rapidly-expanding opening.

Chris leaned inward toward the now symmetrical crevice, all the while keeping a watchful eye on the hovering menace above. Inside the hole, dirt gave way to a faint orange glow and a stench reminiscent of a morgue.

Chris wanted out of there now.

Turning quickly, he moved as fast as his ankle would allow him to. The rope, as if sensing his retreat, crashed down violently, wrapping itself around his legs. Its strength was far superior to any man's, and it had little difficulty in bringing down its opponent.

The knife slipped from Chris's hands as he was hoisted into the air. He watched as his last chance for escape dropped to the ground, its blade gleaming between the leaves. Chris felt his desire to live fading away, his instinct for survival diminishing. The rope was doing it. It would be easier for it to draw its prey down with less resistance.

He passed out seconds before the thing in the ground swallowed him whole.

The rope blindly snaked its way toward the knife. Grasping it tightly, it tossed it into a small hole it has dug nearby. The knife landed next to a bloody baseball cap. Earth was pushed over them, and soon they were completely covered.

Then the rope flopped to the ground to await its next meal.

THE INSTINCT TO SURVIVE

Drake rotated the vertical blinds to see the sunrise. It was part of his morning ritual; a part that he looked forward to more and more with each passing day.

He turned the long white rod and watched as the slotted, plastic strips unanimously opened to reveal the brilliant yellow orb slowly rising in the far horizon.

A smile formed on his face.

On the stove, the teapot was starting to whistle. A thin plume of steam was spewing out of the lid, as the whistle steadily grew louder. Drake quickly retreated to the stove and twisted the gas knob to the *off* position. He removed the lid, being ever so careful not to touch the pot as he had done so so many painful times before. The water beneath the lid furiously roiled about almost as if it were alive. The noise it made was as clear as the rattle of a rattlesnake. It stated loudly for anyone near it to exercise caution.

Drake picked up the pot and poured the bubbling liquid into his brown, oversize coffee mug. The faded happy face with the words *Have a nice day* positioned beneath it stared back at him.

He loved that cup. He'd had it since he first moved here. Its previous owner obviously had used it many times before, hence its worn condition, and Drake planned on using it for quite awhile, or at least until he moved again.

He sipped the tea lightly and contemplated the day. What would he do? He had no job to be at, no obligations to fulfill, no friends or family to visit. He was free as an eagle, soaring high above the collective, chaotic beast of civilization.

He took another drink of tea. The steaming fluid rushed down his throat producing a warm feeling in his gut that extended down through his legs.

But the feeling in his legs was much too strong.

He leaned forward and confirmed the worst: an enormous hole in his abdomen stared back at him. A sickening concoction of green tea and rotten visceral dripped sloppily from the opening.

"The tea must have been too hot," he thought out loud.

Several layers of duct tape sealed the hole satisfactorily and stopped, although only temporarily, the escape of entrails and other internal substances. He concluded that the skin must have become weak due to decomposition. How he let this happen he couldn't explain. He had always been so thorough before. But that never was any guarantee against these types of problems.

He felt like taking a drive. A smooth, calm drive in an automobile always had a relaxing effect on him. He fished the keys out of a cluttered basket by the front door and tossed a baseball cap on his head. He contemplated taking a few CDs but decided it would be too much trouble.

As he strolled out the door he noticed the large safety pin imbedded in his thumb. He pulled it out quickly and wiped the greenish ooze off his hand.

Outside, it was a beautiful day. The sun warmed the ground as the trees danced gently with the wind. Drake began to walk toward the light-blue and slightly rusted Toyota, only to be addressed by a frail, elderly woman who apparently lived next door to him.

"Drake," she mumbled while fiddling with the gardening tools she held in her hands. "You don't look so well." The clothes she wore hung so loosely on her tiny frame that she nearly lost her balance from the wind catching them. "Do you feel all right, my dear?"

Drake looked into her aged eyes. The sincerity in those eyes truly touched him…but only to a small degree.

"Do I know you?" he inquired, not particularly caring what the response would be.

"Why yes. Yes you do. We've lived next door to each other for years. Do you feel okay dear?"

Drake brushed her aside and strolled casually to the Toyota. He considered her for moment but quickly decided she was far too old for his tastes.

Once inside the car he made some minor adjustments to the seat and mirrors. He smashed the radio with his fist when he could not get a station to tune in clearly and then cursed when he had trouble shifting the car into reverse.

The old lady was standing on her lawn with a puzzled expression on her face. She could not understand why her neighbor did not recognize her. Drake paused to look at her. Too old, he mused to himself. Much too old.

Every house resembled the one on either side of it. Each sported somewhat neglected lawns and faded and chipped paint.

Drake dangled his left arm out the window as the warm breeze filtered through his hair. He attempted to relax, to fully embrace and enjoy the ride, but he was troubled. The hole in his gut was not going away. Green liquid seeped through the tape, soaking his lap and the seat. He had to do something about it. He knew it would get only worse.

He began to search. He noticed a woman jogging along the sidewalk. She had on a bright pink sweat suit, which contrasted strongly with her jet-black hair. He eyed an attractive blond woman pushing a frilly baby stroller. She appeared rather young, almost too young to be a mother, and Drake found himself wondering if she even knew who the father was. He glimpsed a teenage boy walking a large dog, his face full of confidence in his canine bodyguard's size.

He had to do something quickly; the injury to his stomach was becoming worse. In addition to that he had another problem that was beginning to manifest itself. A problem he was not accustomed to experiencing. A problem that despite its unfamiliar nature was demanding recognition…guilt. He was actually feeling remorse for what he had done and it gnawed at him like a rat on a bone.

Was he responsible for his deeds or merely a victim? Certainly he had no choice in the matter, but he couldn't lie to himself about not enjoying what he did…at least sometimes.

And then he did something that surprised himself more than it would have surprised anyone who had ever come in contact with him. Something that he even thought he was physically and emotionally incapable of doing: he wept.

He cried loud and hard. A true heartfelt sobbing for all the lives he had affected in any way.

The bright red convertible Corvette caught him completely off guard. The twenty-two year old driver, the son of a successful movie producer, blindsided him viciously, causing the Toyota to roll over twice. When it finally came to a stop, Drake was pinned inside with both his legs crushed. The interior of the car was coated in a sickly green, contrasting grotesquely with the beige seats.

Drake looked up and saw a sea of faces descending on him. The woman jogger in pink, the pretty blond woman with the baby stroller, the teenage boy with his dog, they were all there along with others; all wearing masks of worry, fear, and pity.

A large, dark-skinned man shouted to the others around him to help him pull Drake free of the wreckage. Two other men immediately joined him and began to pry open the twisted remnants of the car's doors. They did not seem to notice or care about the strange green substance in the car.

Drake felt no pain as he drifted in and out of consciousness. He was a limp mannequin subject to the manipulations of his rescuers. He knew death was approaching quickly, and he contemplated staying where he was and letting it finally overtake him. In a way, he was eager to receive it; to drift into its quiet embrace. The peace it offered in its cold grip would be most welcome. But the instinct to survive was also strong and he felt the two feelings do battle in his mind.

And then darkness overtook the light.

The woman jogger in pink resumed her exercise, her morbid curiosity satisfied and content in the fact that she could do nothing to help.

The pretty blonde woman continued on her way, pushing the stroller along while humming softly to the baby inside of it. She did her best to calm the infant's tiny mind and to soothe its little ears from the destruction all around it.

And the teenage boy with his oversize dog moved on as well. He needed to get home and feed the dog, as well as do his homework.

The dog growled and gnashed its teeth, throwing its head from side to side violently. It was angry. It had stepped on a jagged stone, which had been concealed under a small pile of leaves causing a nasty cut on its front paw.

The teenage boy was shocked and worried at his dog's behavior. The dog had never acted like that before. He knelt down and tried to console his pet. The dog seemed okay but was still very aggressive and agitated as if it didn't recognize its owner.

The teenage boy looked at the dog's paw. The wound was a serious one, approximately two inches long and somewhat deep. The teenage boy was very worried; he did not know what the strange green substance coming out of the cut was.

CHANGES IN APPETITE

"Of course I feel fine," Rick Jerith moaned as the doctor poked and prodded his body for the umpteenth time in the last two days. His irritation from feeling like a lab rat was beginning to show through every word he spoke. "I really don't see any need for this, Doc."

Doctor Maisan, a small, soft-spoken man in his early sixties, continued with his examination. His fascination with his patient's unique and thoroughly unprecedented situation drove his tireless efforts to unlock what had actually happened two days earlier.

"I'm going to require a urine sample," Doctor Maisan stated in a sterile tone. "And perhaps another blood sample as well." He glanced up at his increasingly annoyed patient. "If that's all right with you, Mr. Jerith."

Rick glared at the doctor. "Fine," he grumbled through clenched teeth. "Whatever. Just make it quick."

Doctor Maisan could hardly contain his excitement. His good fortune of being the one and only doctor in the tiny, isolated town of Newsbury, Michigan was almost too good to be true. Of all the towns, in all the counties, he, Dr. Coleman A. Maisan, practiced in the one place where a young man actually rose from his casket during his funeral and announced he was not dead after all. He himself had pronounced the man dead after examining him thoroughly, and now here was the same man sitting in his office claiming that he felt perfectly normal.

"How many more tests do you have to do?" Rick asked. He was starting to get hungry and wanted nothing more than to head back to his little disorganized house and lose himself in various television channels. "I know what happened to me was really weird, but I feel fine. In fact, I feel great." He flexed his large arms to emphasize his point.

"I know, I know Mr. Jerith," Doctor Maisan replied quietly while selecting a large specimen container from a drawer. "But I need you to fill this up for me if you would."

Rick glared at the plastic cup. "That thing is huge. How am I supposed to fill that up?"

"Just do the best you can please," Doctor Maisan said with a smile. "And then we can discuss your situation a little."

Rick frowned. "I already told you what happened. I was working on my roof, and I slipped coming down the ladder. I guess the patio cement broke my fall."

"Yes. I believe you broke your neck. I examined you myself."

Rick just shrugged. "Yeah, I guess I did, but I feel great now. Look." He swung his head back and forth, twisting it in all directions.

Doctor Maisan nodded. "Yes, yes I know. It's perfectly normal now." He set down the needle he was preparing. "Rather fascinating I might add. No sign of damage whatsoever, not even any bruising." An expression of worry crossed his weathered face. "To be honest, Mr. Jerith…I'm baffled."

Rick laughed. "I'll tell ya something really strange though doc. I feel better now than before I had the accident…much, much better."

Doctor Maisan smiled nervously. "Have you had any other changes worth noting, such as sleeping habits or a change in appetite?"

Rick's smile grew wider. The sterile white glow from the light fixtures reflected off his eyes. "Nope. Still sleep like a baby, and my appetite…is…ahhh. My appetite…"

A cold lump formed in Doctor Maisan's throat. "Yes Mr. Jerith? What about your appetite?"

"My appetite has changed a little now that you mention it doc," Rick slurred, thick drool cascading down his chest. "Lately, I've had this huge craving for…brains."

BELIEVE

    Tyler sat in his bed, huddled under his blankets, glaring down at his bedroom floor. A thin layer of sweat coated his body, making him feel very uncomfortable. How he hated that sticky, wet feeling. It reminded him of when he had a fever, drained of all of his energy and full of aches and pains. In a strange way however, he wished the sweat *were* from a fever. That would have been preferable to the real cause of it, which was from simply being nervous.

    Tyler gripped his blanket tightly, attempting to extract as much false security from it as he could. Nearby, his baseball bat, the same one he'd smacked a home run with the week before, leaned against the bedpost, silently offering its assistance if it was needed.

    Tyler's thoughts drifted back to his friend Joey and what he had said when they camped out in his parent's backyard a few nights before.

    In the yellow glow of his flashlight, Joey had pulled out a small, leather-bound book from beneath his pillow. He went on to explain that it was his father's, and he had accidentally found it in his basement the week before. It was hidden with other curious items in tightly bound boxes hidden behind the furnace. His dad always had been interested in weird occult stuff, and had amassed quite a collection of the stuff.

    "There's no title on it," Joey pointed out. "But if you look on the first page near the bottom you'll see a single word scratched into the paper. It says... *Believe*."
He then flipped open the book and motioned toward the otherwise blank first page. There, almost unreadable, was a single word sloppily written in dark red ink. Tyler leaned forward.

    "It says... *Believe*," Joey repeated as if reading his friend's mind. "That's what it says."

    Tyler felt his spine stiffen as a cold sweat tightened its uncomfortable grip on his body. He looked down at the floor of his bedroom and noticed dozens of footprints littering the carpet.

Some were large, as if from grown men and women, while others were comparably small, apparently from children. They were scattered everywhere, and criss-crossed each other frequently. Tyler knew very well what they were and who had made them.

Dead people.

They were made by whole families, by wandering loners, by lost souls with no place to rest. And all forgotten and long dead.

"You wanna see something really weird?" Joey had asked on that ill-fated night in the tent. "Check this out." He then proceeded to flip through the remaining pages in the book, pausing briefly on each one. "You see that?" he asked as a smile slid across his face. "They're all the same. The same word on every page: *Believe*."

"But why? And what does it mean?" Tyler had asked, although he didn't really want to know.

Joey looked at his friend with a glint in his eye. "All you have to do is read every page out loud."

"Is that all?" Tyler had remarked sarcastically.

Joey laughed. "No, not really. You have to *believe* each time you say it." He then closed the book and opened his fourth can of soda pop. "But I have to warn you though," he continued. "there are some things you don't want to believe in."

Joey had always been a strange character, and Tyler sometimes wondered just why they were such good friends.

"Fine," Tyler said to his friend. "Give me the stupid book. I'll read every dumb page." He was surprised at his courage sometimes.

"Suit yourself," Joey replied. "But your life might change a little." He smiled and took a swig of his soda. "I know mine did."

Tyler cursed at himself as he recalled flipping through every page in the book and saying the words loud and clear. He had followed Joey's instructions exactly, reciting each word while looking directly at it and clearing his mind of any distractions. Only the word itself and its meaning occupied his thoughts. And most important of all, he actually convinced himself to believe in the words and the book.

But none of that mattered now as he sat on his bed, alone and scared. In the last few days he'd seen things that were weird and very disturbing, things which should not be seen.

First, there was the pretty young woman hovering over his school bus. Her face, stained with the blood of her death, was twisted by pain and anger. Then there was the tall man standing in the middle of an aisle in the grocery store, bruises covering his swollen body, head bent so far back it looked as if it would fall off. Apparently, he had suffered a broken neck in some type of accident.

And there were many others as well. Bloody, mangled bodies and faces, distorted features, expressions of stark terror and pain. Some appeared almost normal, while others were nothing more than shells of people. And then there was when he made the mistake of walking past Hollowthorn Cemetery. The noises he'd heard coming from the ground gave him nightmares. Terrible scratching sounds like the dead were trying to claw their way out of their graves.

And they all had one thing in common…

all were directed at him, as if they knew he was aware of them. It was as if they were always there, but until truly believed in could not fully exist.

Tyler grit his teeth in fear. The pale moonlight, which streamed into his room casting shadows everywhere, further heightened the tension that already paralyzed him. Joey's words danced in his head. *There are things you don't want to know. Your life might change a little.* Now Tyler knew what those words meant.

He looked down at his bedroom floor again and realized that his situation could be much worse than he previously thought. He always had an active imagination, something he thought would have been an asset in his life, but now it seemed to make his problems worse. It allowed him to enter fantastic lands and see strange creatures. In a way, he actually believed in these worlds within his mind. He was the master, creating things the way he thought they should or would be. The escapism his imagination offered was priceless to him. Troubles at school or with girls could not enter these lands, and although they waited for him back in reality he still enjoyed his creations whenever possible.

But that is what caused his problems as well. By believing in them, even if only for a minute, and by reading the strange book from his friend Joey, he gave life to them.

And ghosts were only the first things to manifest themselves in his world…and certainly not the most frightening.

Tyler looked at the footprints on the floor of his bedroom. The ghosts had been everywhere, even walking around before his house had been built. They left tracks for a true believer like Tyler to see. But there were other tracks as well, made from things which weren't human, and never had been. Born in his imagination, and since believed in at one time or another, anxious to explore their new world. They were long, distorted things slithering around in all directions, blotting out many of the ghostly footprints. He watched in horror as new ones appeared right before his eyes. Twisted, snakelike tracks, searching for something to believe in them, to make them real.

Tyler's stomach churned when some of the tracks turned toward him, and appearing to hesitate for a moment or two, began to approach his bed. His imagination raced in an attempt to create creatures that would make such tracks; at least if he knew what they were he might be able to deal with them better.

Slowly, the things began to appear, excited with hunger and their newfound capacity to feed. They had existed in Tyler's mind for too long, and were now quite anxious to test their abilities.

They gathered in growing numbers and surrounded the frightened young boy on his bed

THE SPEED DEMON

Frank took a sip from his rapidly-cooling coffee. Sometimes he thought if he only had one wish in the world it would be for a better cup of coffee that never cooled down.

Wishful thinking for a bored police officer baking in his hot patrol car.

The waiting was the hardest part of his job. Passing endless hours under the blazing sun in a dust bowl like Sturgell, Nebraska, waiting for speeders was definitely not one of the best parts of his career. He often felt like a caged rat, trapped behind the steering wheel of the black and white 1992 Corsica that came with his paycheck. The radio offered little more than distraction, and frequently tossed in static for good measure. And the sun did its best to make the landscape dry and the air uncomfortable and difficult to breathe.

"Doubt we'll get anyone today," he mumbled to the interior of his car. "Nothing happening. Nothing at all."

It worried Frank sometimes when he talked to himself. He didn't want to end up like his father, struggling to maintain his sanity and his bank account, but found that hearing his own voice usually eased the loneliness and boredom.

One hour drifted into the next, each indistinguishable from the one before it. Sleep tempted him with its promise of comfort, but Frank resisted. He knew he needed to stay awake, just in case some kids came speeding by.

The noise was small at first, almost inaudible, but it was enough to pull Frank from his peaceful daydream.

"What's this?" he whispered to himself. "Is there finally someone coming?"

He removed his dust-coated sunglasses and squinted at the horizon. There, nearly too small to see, was a tiny black dot racing toward him, slowly but steadily gaining in size as it drew nearer. The distinct whine of its engine was literally an open invitation to a bored and weary police officer trying to meet his monthly quota of tickets.

Frank watched anxiously as the black dot grew in size. Whoever it was they were definitely speeding. Frank felt a small fire of excitement begin to smolder in his gut. It was held in check by his oath to uphold the law, but he still felt it burn nonetheless. After all, this was just what he was waiting for.

He reached over and picked up his hand-held radar gun. Switching it on quickly, he punched in the necessary settings and waited to clock the speed demon barreling down the road towards him. The target speed range of the gun was excellent, one of the best on the market, and Frank let a smile creep across his dusty, sun-baked face when he thought about it.

"I wonder what type of car it is," he mumbled to no one. "Gotta be something nice to be going as fast as it is. Maybe a Corvette, or one of those old Ford hot rods, all souped up with big-block motors and thick, illegal tires.

Illegal. The very sound of the word excited Frank. Job security was what it was all about, and illegal activities were his bread and butter. As long as there were people doing things they shouldn't be doing he'd have a paycheck.

Frank glanced at the display on the radar gun. It blinked on and off a few times, switching between 148 and 153, before finally settling more or less on 151.

Taking a deep breath and exhaling, Frank let the number run through his mind. He'd never come across someone going that fast. This was gonna be a really good ticket, maybe with reckless driving thrown in for good measure.

Setting the radar gun down Frank unbuckled his firearm and twisted the ignition key. The patrol car came to life with the steady hum of the engine, which elicited a smile from Frank. He was finally going to have some action today.

"Now all we have to do is wait until he comes by," he mused to himself. "Then we got him."

The speeding car continued barreling down the road, apparently oblivious to the police car waiting for it to pass by. It was picking up speed, nearing 155 miles per hour, and putting anything or anyone in its way in extreme danger.

Frank depressed the brake pedal and shifted the car into drive. He gripped the steering wheel with both hands and waited for the speed demon to liven up his day.

It happened so fast Frank barely realized it. A blur would have been the best way to describe it, or perhaps a smear of paint like in a crazy abstract painting. The car was moving so fast that it hardly resembled a car at all. It could have been a giant bird for all he could tell.

Flipping his sirens and lights on, Frank pulled his foot off the brake pedal and slammed it down on the accelerator. The car's tires spun furiously, kicking up a small dust storm and propelling the vehicle out onto the weathered asphalt. Frank struggled to straighten it out, but eventually succeeded and begun his pursuit of the speeding car.

Apparently, the speeder noticed the flashing lights behind him and immediately slowed down. Within a minute he came to a dusty stop off the side of the road.

Frank couldn't believe his eyes when he stepped out of his patrol car and finally got a good look at the car. He had expected a Corvette or Mustang, or maybe a classic muscle car. Or at the very least some type of nice automobile. But what he saw instead hardly passed for a car at all, much less any hot rod street machine capable of 150 miles per hour.

It was a red Chevy Malibu, mid to late 70's if he had to guess, mostly held together by rust and rubber bands. The tires were pencil thin and as bald as a newborn baby, and the body had so many dents it looked as if it had been in at least a dozen accidents.

Frank adjusted his hat, and resting his right hand on his firearm, proceeded to approach the vehicle slowly. In his left hand he held a thick pack of tickets and a pen.

"Do you have any idea how fast you were going?"
No response.
"Can I see your driver's license and registration please?"
Again, no response.

The driver of the car, a teenage boy with dirty blond hair hanging down to his scrawny shoulders, merely stared straight ahead wearing a look of stupidity that bordered on mental deficiency. His clothes were filthy and Frank could practically see his ribs protruding out of his torso. He looked as if he hadn't eaten in days.

"Son, I'll need your driver's license and registration please," Frank repeated with a bit of compassion, something he usually didn't afford speeders. But the kid continued to stare straight ahead, completely oblivious to Frank or his situation.

"Step out of the car… please!" Frank stated in a dull tone. His patience was running thin and he was starting to think the kid might be on something.

But still no response.

Although he didn't want to Frank felt compelled to pull out his gun. He took a few steps back, spread his legs and leveled his weapon at the kid.

"I said out of the car now!"

The kid cocked his head to the side a little and looked at Frank. He then calmly opened his door and stepped out onto the dusty road, his featureless expression never changing. Frank whirled the kid around and pulled his thin arms behind his back. Within thirty seconds he had his handcuffs on and had patted him down.

"You're under arrest, punk," he growled. "Speeding, reckless driving, resisting an officer…"

Frank's words were cut off by a heavy thumping sound coming from the trunk of the car. Instantly, images of tightly bound captives of some bizarre kidnapping plot ran across his mind. "What's in the trunk?" he asked while tapping his gun.

The kid lifted his head up off the car, and swinging it around to push the hair out of his face, locked his eyes on Frank. The thirty seconds he stared at Frank passed like hours, culminating in a greasy smile that obviously hid a secret.

Frank's attention was finally broken by the increasingly loud noises from the trunk of the car. They were growing in volume and occasionally were accompanied by soft groans, as if someone were gagged and in pain. Frank wasted no time in depositing the kid in the back seat of his patrol car and briskly, yet carefully, walked over to the trunk of the car. Despite holding his gun in his hand he was still uneasy about how the situation could escalate.

The trunk lid lifted violently as the occupant inside beat against it. Frank's hands trembled, and despite the dry air he found himself sweating.

"Hello, I'm a police officer. Stay calm and I'll get you out," Frank said as he glanced back at his patrol car. The kid was still in the backseat wearing a foolish grin and sitting perfectly still. His look gave Frank the creeps.

To Frank's surprise the trunk lid opened fairly easily, releasing a pungent odor that instantly wrapped itself around his nose. Pulling his handkerchief from his pocket, he covered his mouth and peered into the trunk.

There, bundled near a bald spare tire and rusty toolbox, was a young, dark-haired teenage girl. She looked up at Frank with tear-stained, bloodshot eyes. Her hair and face were crusted with dried blood, and bruises covered her neck. Frank wasted no time and quickly pulled the thick gag out of her tiny mouth. She spit some blood and a tooth out as she gasped for air.

"Take it easy, young lady," Frank consoled. "I'll have ya outta here in a second."

"Take your time, officer," she slurred with a smile. "I have all day."

The unusual response caught Frank off guard. He paused from releasing her bonds and stared at her. His blood froze in his veins when the girl started to melt into the trunk, leaving only an oily residue behind.

"W...what the..." were the only words Frank was able to get out before the trunk lid, which had sprouted four-inch serrated teeth, slammed shut, cleanly slicing him in two at the waist. The lower part of his body fell to the ground in a bloody heap, twitching a few times before settling onto the road.

The kid slid out of the handcuffs and kicked the patrol car's door open. He sauntered over to where Frank's remains were, and hoisting them up over his shoulder, promptly lifted the trunk lid and tossed them in, eliciting a deep, guttural purr from the car.

The kid then strolled back to the front of the car and crawled into the driver's seat. His body began to melt, oozing right into the seat, leaving only his upper torso intact. He tapped the steering wheel once and the 1977 Chevy Malibu rumbled to life, leaving a cloud of dust behind it as it pulled out onto the road. It then sped off into the distance looking for its next meal.

IN THE DARK

I never feared the dark.

Most kids my age at the time did though, displaying tough-guy exteriors and then huddling under the false security of their blankets at night.

But not me. I embraced the dark. I guess it had something to do with it allowing me to hide from my problems. It shielded me from other's perception of how I should be or how I should act. It permitted me to become whatever, or whomever, I wished to be.

Yes, I liked the dark, or at least I did until I joined the Cub Scouts.

David Green was a good friend. The scout meetings we had were always at his house because his mother was our scout leader. We would go over different building projects, ways to raise money for the group, and talk about upcoming events. And sometimes we would play games as well.

I still remember the day when Mrs. Green told us about a new game she invented for the group. She said something about getting the idea for it in a dream, a dream that seemed to come to her in different sections over several nights. Eventually she pieced together enough of her dreams to form the basis for the game.

And it was called *In the Dark*.

The object of the game was to guess what was in certain bowls just by inserting your hands into them. I know it sounds lame, but to a bunch of hyped-up ten year-olds it was something really cool. Mrs. Green would put some really strange stuff in some of the bowls like spaghetti, meatloaf and pea soup. Sometimes she even used grass clippings or cooking oil.

We first played it during our Halloween party one year. Mrs. Green had the basement decked out real nice with scary decorations and candy everywhere, and all us kids were really excited about playing the new game. I wore my pirate costume, which everyone said made me look like Blackbeard. I thought that was funny because his real name wasn't Blackbeard, it was Edward Teach.

The stairs were in the center of the basement so there were basically two separate sections, the laundry room and storage area and the main entertainment area. Mrs. Green closed the slotted door to the laundry room behind her as she disappeared into the darkness to prepare the game. After what seemed like an eternity she finally emerged from the room and announced that the first recipient could come forward.

I remember thinking what a strange thing to call a player in a game. Recipient?

Mrs. Green shuffled back into the room for a moment or two and then poked herd head out of the door, adding, "I'm sure you kids will love my new game."

The chill I felt at her words was lost on me at the time, but now, unfortunately for me, I know better.

"It's very simple," she explained. "Each of you goes into that room," she gestured toward the laundry room door, "and sit yourselves down in the chair in the middle of the room. There will be a series of bowls set out on a table in front of the chair. When I tell you to, put one of your hands into one of the bowls. Do it slowly so you don't spill anything." Her face grew flush with excitement. "If you can guess correctly what's in the bowl you win a prize and advance to the next level. But you only get two guesses."

I remember entertaining wild thoughts about what could be in the bowls. Intestines, mashed spiders, cooked brains, raw sewage. The possibilities were endless for a ten year-old's mind.

"I'll give you one clue though," Mrs. Green added. "Each bowl contains something edible." And with that vague but intriguing clue, she trotted back into the laundry room. Her voice rang through the door a few seconds later. "Give me a minute and then I'll call for one of you."

I had already decided by that time that I wasn't going to be the first one to go in. I wasn't afraid of the dark, just what might be in it.

"John Welch, please," Mrs. Green then called out from behind the door.

John, another good friend of mine, bravely strutted up to the door, and looking back as if to verify that he was not afraid, strolled into the darkness.

After what seemed like an eternity, he walked out of the laundry room sporting a huge grin. In his right hand he held a small towel and in his left was a brand new Action Paction Space Figure, still in the package.

"All right!" he exclaimed. "I won! I won!"

We all gathered around him, trying to find out what information we could.

"I guessed it on the first try," he boasted. "It was oatmeal."

Mrs. Green then emerged from the room. She was nearly as excited as John was. "Okay kids," she said with a smile. "Give me a minute and I'll call in another." And then she disappeared through the door again.

John was too busy trying to tear open his prize to be bothered with our questions. I merely stood back and plotted what I would do if I were called next.

"David. David Green."

David looked over at me wearing an expression like it was Christmas morning. Without saying a word he strolled through the door, confident his mother would grant him victory.

I remember entertaining the thought of which prize I would prefer if I won. But what would be in the bowls? And what if they contained something that wasn't edible? What if there were body parts or mashed spiders in them? What if Mrs. Green wasn't really the kindly woman she pretended to be?

Looking back now I feel a little foolish for thinking like that, but I was just a kid at the time. If only I knew then what was going to happen I wouldn't have gone into that room in the first place.

David Green came strolling out of the laundry room door grinning. He too had a brand new Action Paction toy in his hands.

"I guessed it was pizza. I knew it was because I felt the pepperonis."

I watched him mingle between the other kids. I was happy for him, as I was for John, but deep inside I was still dreading when my name would be called.

And eventually, it was.

I was prodded toward the door of the laundry room by the other kids. Virtually all of them had some type of gift from the game, leaving me to feel left out. I let myself be nudged along as I gradually approached the pitch-black rectangle of the laundry room. Mrs. Green's voice rang out from the darkness, coaxing me into the mysteries of the new game.

"Come on now, Honey," Mrs. Green said sweetly. "Just follow my voice and you'll locate the chair in the center of the room. Seat yourself down and wait for me to give you further instructions."

I stumbled into the darkness, occasionally bumping into a wall before I found the chair and sat down. I was nervous, but also excited.

"Okay dear, now put one of your hands into the bowl on the right." I heard her shuffle back and forth a bit, and clear her throat. "You can keep it in the bowl for as long as you like, but you only get two guesses as to what it might be."

I decided not to hesitate, and put my right hand into the bowl in front of me, sliding it into the cold, oily mixture up to the wrist.

"Can you tell me what it is?"

I thought for a moment, swirling my hand around in the bowl, but could not think of what it might be. "I don't know," I finally admitted.

"That's okay," Mrs. Green consoled. "you still get one more try."

I heard her move the bowl in front of me over and promptly slide another one into its place. Again I pushed my hand into the bowl. The substance was warm and fairly thick in consistency.

"Mashed potatoes?" I ventured without hesitating.

"That's right!" Mrs. Green cried. "Congratulations! You've made it to the second round. I'll get you your prize."

I felt a small towel tossed into my lap. The relief I felt was overwhelming, not only because I'd won, but also because I could then leave that dark room. But as I was standing up a strange thought slipped into my mind:

What if it wasn't mashed potatoes?

My curiosity took over, and in the next instant I found myself reaching for the light switch. I needed to see what was in that bowl.

I found the switch and quickly flipped it up.

The room was instantly flooded with light. I focused on the two bowls on the table where I had been seated at only a minute before. The one on the left contained a familiar substance, some type of salad dressing, but the other one held something that to this day I still can't identify.

It was deep gray in color and generously sprinkled with tiny specks of dirty yellow lumps. I stared in awe at the dreadful stuff, not really sure if I were imagining it or not. I could have sworn that I even saw one of the grotesque little lumps move. It swirled around in the filthy mixture, leaving tiny trails behind it.

But even that wasn't the worst of it. Glancing up I caught a glimpse of a figure crouching in the corner of the room behind the water heater. I say *figure* because whatever it was didn't resemble a human being in any way. An oversize fly would have been a better description.

And then in a flash it was gone, scurrying out of sight behind the water heater. The voice that followed carved an icy slit in my soul forever.

"Turn that light off now!" Mrs. Green's voice demanded. "Do you hear me young man?" She then walked out from behind the water heater wearing an annoyed expression on her face.

I switched the light switch off.

"Here's your prize," she said sternly while ushering me out of the room. Her grip was like steel and incredibly cold. "But if you don't follow the rules you'll be sent home. Do I make myself clear?"

To this day I vividly recall Mrs. Green's eyes at the time. They were like clear, glass marbles, void of any emotion, any compassion, any humanity. I was pushed into the basement where the other kids were waiting.

"What's that stuff on your hand?" David Green asked me.

"I...I don't know," I stuttered. "It was what was in one of the bowls. I..."

At that minute Mrs. Green came back into the room. She was wiping her hands on a towel and glaring at me. I didn't know what to say, so I just slouched my shoulders and stared at the floor.

The remainder of the party went by quickly, and I eventually left by myself.

While walking home I noticed that my hand was feeling somewhat tingly, like tiny needles were jabbing into the flesh. I looked at it closely, but saw nothing out of the ordinary except for a little swelling. It subsided within a few hours, but still left me with an uneasy feeling as to what caused it in the first place.

I quit the Scouts the next week. I told my parents, and myself, that it was because of other interests I had, but the real reason was that I wanted to get away from Mrs. Green and that house. I hardly talked to David Green after that, both of us hanging out with other friends. I felt bad about it, but I didn't want to take any chances.

I tried not to think about the Halloween party after that, but I often did. I attempted to lock those images from that day away in the back of my mind, slamming the door on them once and for all. But in a strange way what transpired that day actually boosted my self-esteem. I'd seen, or thought I did, something frightening, and I dealt with it in my own way.

Twenty years have passed now. Come to think of it, exactly twenty years tomorrow since that Halloween party at David Green's house. I'm planning on
camping out on the front porch tonight, just to make sure no punks damage any of my property, but this stomach ache is killing me. Sometimes it feels like I'm gonna split wide open.

Walonda took Bobby to the store. She's picking up some last minute decorations and his costume. Bobby can't wait for the Halloween party we're giving him tomorrow night. He's gonna be a pirate, maybe Blackbeard.

I told Walonda that…that…

It will be tough but I know I can have things ready in time. You see, I'm gonna show the kids at the party tomorrow night a new game. I just know they'll love it. I know they've never played anything like *In the Dark* before.

FLOWER IN THE WIND

Paula watched as tiny pebbles and dirt cascaded down from high above, creating an empty symphony in the cave. The echoes reverberated throughout the space, and although she had grown mildly accustomed to them, they still affected her in many ways. They tapped into her mind trying to fracture the delicate barrier between sanity and insanity.

Occasionally a stray memory wandered into her conscience and struggled for validity but fought against the erosion of time, which substantially diluted each and every one regardless of their sentimentality or importance.

The memory that most steadfastly attempted to be recognized and appreciated was of her fiancé Tom. She could still see his wavy blond hair and crystal blue eyes, she could still smell his masculine and attractive aroma, she could still hear his soft but confident voice say I love you. All of these things still remained in her mind and were her only connection to her comfortable and loving past, a past that was slipping away like a flower in the wind.

The wind. She shuddered at the thought of it. It was the cause of the catastrophic situation she, and very likely the rest of the world, was in. High, relentless, gusty winds; and not just normal gales but mind-numbing, destructive and all-encompassing ones, enveloping all before them in an indiscriminatory embrace of devastation.

She walked towards the opening of the cave and carefully pulled out a small oval- shaped stone from the hastily constructed wall that she and the others had assembled. Instantly, the ear-splitting howls of the wind permeated the cave. Peering out displayed only what she already knew: a vast and featureless terrain.

"Smooth as glass," the voice behind her said. It was Roy. His six-foot frame towered over her petite form, and he outweighed her by at least fifty pounds. "Nothing left out there but flat land…and the wind of course."

She whirled around to face him. His pockmarked face, from a severe bout with chicken pox when he was a young boy, glared down at her. A wry smile slid across his features like water in a bucket of oil.

"Roy, do you mind?" she said sternly. She knew that he coveted her love and had even gotten into a drunken brawl with Tom once over her. She also knew that she must be careful. Tom was not around to protect her anymore.

Roy stood in her way. He used his size to intimidate others, which was one of the many traits that she detested in him. She had wished many times that he would have been swept away by the wind instead of Tom. but unfortunately that was not the case.

"Becky needs me; I have to change the dressing on her wounds." She brushed past him as quickly as she could, being careful not to anger him, that would only complicate the dire situation they were already in.

There was only him, his teenage cousin Becky and Louise, a neighbor girl who happened to be riding her bike by Paula's house when the worst gales started to hit. She had managed to escape with them just in time.

"Paula," Becky moaned in a weak voice. "Will you come here please? I'm very thirsty." The dark corner where she lay was full of rocks and crawled with bugs. Paula felt bad for her and wished there was a more comfortable spot for her. She scurried over to Becky and began to collect the small, dirty plastic cups they had scattered around the cave to gather water. What little water trickled down from the ceiling barely was enough to sustain one person, much less four. She gave the cups to Becky, who greedily sucked them down.

"Why bother with her?" Roy growled. "You know as well as I do she's not gonna make it."

"She's your cousin!" Paula shouted back.

Roy grit his teeth and scowled, "I don't give a crap if she's Marilyn Monroe, we shouldn't be wasting water on her! She's not gonna make it!"

Paula reared back and slapped him. She immediately regretted it, not because he didn't deserve it but because she realized that they could not afford to fight amongst themselves. They needed to work together if they were going to survive.

Roy stared at her. The red mark across his face glared brightly and contrasted strongly with his pale skin. But to her surprise and relief he simply walked away. Becky looked up at Paula, tears streaming down her battered face.

"He's right you know," she whispered. "you shouldn't waste time on me."

Paula bent down and gave her a hug. "Don't worry. We'll get through this."

*   *   *   *

The broken anemometer sat near the cave's entrance. She had managed to grab it at the last minute and threw it in her bag. Why she did she didn't know, other than it might be the only part of her little brother Joey that she had left.

He had been an amateur meteorologist of sorts and had several devices used for measuring and observing weather conditions. She fondly recalled him spewing out various information about topics regarding weather. He had bought the anemometer through a catalog and had altered it to be very accurate with his own parts. He added gauges and fittings and cups to the existing ones and painted it a bright red. It was one of his most cherished pieces of equipment.

The dial he added gave a clear and fairly accurate reading of wind speed. She had fastened it to the ground just outside the cave when they had first arrived and had pulled it back in before it blew away. She looked at the gauge. The glass was cracked badly but the reading was still legible: one-hundred and two miles per hour, and that was a few days ago; the gusts had increased rapidly and steadily since then. She guessed they were probably near one hundred and fifty miles per hour, perhaps more.

"Kinda tempting isn't it?" Roy's voice seemed to emanate from the darkness itself. "Just to walk out into the wind and let it take you. Ya get to see the world." His face appeared in the blackness followed by the remainder of his body. "It'll be like flying, soaring as high as you could wanna go."

Paula steadied her nerves as best she could. "You're tired Roy," she reasoned. "You need some rest. I'll get you a blanket." She reached for her bag and withdrew a tattered quilt that her mother had sewn when she was a little girl. Roy rushed forward and seized her wrist.

"We could go together. Imagine it, the two of us flying high, seeing the world," he said.

She yanked her arm from his grasp. "You need some sleep," she retorted angrily and walked back to her spot in the cave. She could feel his eyes watching her, and knew very well that he was beginning to lose his mind.

Sleep did its best to elude her but sheer exhaustion, both physically and mentally, eventually won out as she fell into a deep and troubled slumber. She dreamt of Tom pulling his truck into her driveway to pick her up for a date. She dreamt of her father working on his hot rod in the garage. She dreamt of her mother cooking up her famous tuna casserole. She dreamt of her brother Joey excitingly running around the house when his latest piece of equipment came in the mail. She even dreamt of Fred, her bloodhound, wiling away the days on the front porch. She dreamt of all these things from her past that were unmistakably tainted with the painful stain of reality.

Her sleep was broken by the sound of stones crumbling. She jerked awake and flung her gaze towards the entranceway of the cave. Roy was there, standing directly in front of the wall and carefully, almost delicately, removing stones from it. He already had several smaller rocks tossed aside and was working on dislodging a large one from the center, as the howls of the wind were beginning to permeate the cave, causing the ceiling to rain down dirt and pebbles.

Paula leapt to her feet and ran to him screaming for him to stop. "Roy what are you doing?" she cried. "You'll kill us all!" She could hear the gusts of wind grow stronger as it tried to enter through any opening it could.

Roy easily pushed her to the ground and increased his effort in removing the large stone. "I'm gonna see the world," he laughed. "Top of the world Ma, I'm gonna be on top of the world!"

Paula grabbed a grapefruit sized rock and flung it with all her might at Roy. Her aim proved good and it landed squarely on the back of his head. He collapsed to the ground cursing at her. Paula realizing the opportunity scuttled over to where he lay and frantically began pulling her shoelaces out to tie him up with. But the wall had been compromised by Roy's efforts and started to crumble right before her eyes.

"You dumb broad," Roy hissed through bloody teeth. "I want to fly, do you hear me? I want to fly!" He reached up and grabbed Paula's ankle and flipped her onto her back. The blood was literally pouring from his wound coating both of them in a sticky mess of crimson. "I'll teach you to stop me," he growled.

He stood up, and digging his hands into the wall, yanked out a large stone near the center. The wind immediately whipped in through the opening and flung everything, including Paula, Louise, and Becky against the back wall of the cave. Roy hung on and began to crawl through the hole. The sight of his skin being peeled back like a ripe piece of fruit was too much for Paula to bear; she buried her and the girl's faces in the blanket. She made the mistake however, of looking up one last time just when Roy reached the outside of the cave and was sucked away with such force that he did not even have time to make a sound. She forced her way back to the wall. Her face and hands stung terribly from the wind and she could feel the blood begin to cover her but she managed to reach the wall and push the rock back into place. Thirty exhaustive minutes later she had the only barrier between them and death reasonably rebuilt and secure.

Behind her she could hear Becky and Louise crying. As if the situation they were in were not bad enough they also had the loss of loved ones haunting their feelings. But at least Roy was gone, of that much they could be grateful for.

Paula walked over to the girls. She wasn't their mother, or even a friend, but she knew she had to be the one to be strong if they were going to survive. Cradling their heads in her arms she joined them in sobbing.

*   *   *   *

Hours passed with no lessoning of the wind. It continued to relentlessly swirl and gust in a song of nature promising death. It had flattened everything in sight to a smooth, featureless plain, void of civilization. The incredible power it displayed was beyond anyone's comprehension or understanding. It was controlling the Earth, tossing aside puny humans at its whim.

Paula sat up and wondered if there was anything left of the outside world. She knew there must be an explanation for the wind. There was little doubt in her mind that there were many scientists and researchers who could easily explain it, but that was of little comfort to her or the girls, or any of the people who had been wiped out. Would they be able to stop it? She doubted it. How could someone stop high winds, especially ones that reached hundreds of miles per hour? Nothing built by man could withstand such a pounding onslaught.

She looked over at Becky and Louise; they were fast asleep next to one another behind her. Their faces masked the pain and fear that she knew lurked below the surface. They were both so young, much younger than she was, and like her they still had so much to live for.

And then she heard it. It was faint almost to the point of being non-existent, but it was definitely there; a low, soft voice…Tom's voice, and it was calling her name…from outside the wall.

"Pauuullaa. Paulaaa, it's me Tom."

The wind diluted the clarity of the words greatly but she was still able to decipher them.

"Are you in there Paula? Pauullaaa…"

Torn between the joy of hearing his voice and common sense, Paula felt herself crawl toward the entranceway of the cave. Becky and Louise were still sound asleep and oblivious to the impending danger they faced, otherwise they surely would have tried to stop her.

She reached the wall and began to remove a small stone near the top. Logic and the instinct to survive were pushed aside by her longing to see her beloved fiancé again, to hold him in her arms and to kiss his lips once more. Dehydration constricted her throat making it nearly impossible to utter a response to the voice other than a low groaning.

"Paauullaaa. Paauullaaa…"

Any hint of malevolence in the words was masked by the source of them. Her finance, the man who she was going to escape with to the big city and pursue her dream of having a family with and attending college. The man she was going to spend the rest of her life with as Mrs. Thomas Kannery. The man she was going to grow old with.

"Paaulla…I'm here. It's me Tom."

Against her better judgment she pulled the small stone out.

Hesitation gripped her mind, momentarily causing her to pause in looking out of the opening. She was scared. However, she was also surprised at how well she had dealt with the situation so far and had faith in herself that she never had before. She had also developed a special bond with the two girls and felt a responsibility for them.

And then she looked out of the hole.

The wind hissed in her face with a ferocity that was terrible to behold. It was still an unyielding behemoth of Nature unmatched by all before it. Shielding her eyes as best she could, Paula strained to see the outside world.

At first, nothing was visible, only the roiling, empty void of nothingness that had cursed her eyes and mind so many times before. But then, an image appeared. A vague silhouette of a face materialized approximately five feet from the wall. Gradually a body formed beneath the face and melted into it giving it a full image of a person.

It was Tom, her beloved fiancé who had been taken by the wind! He looked at her and smiled a loving and familiar smile.

"Hello Paula," he said through the assault from the wind, which was whipping his blond hair all about his face.

She was speechless; words failed her completely. The impossibility of what she was seeing was matched only by her desire for it to be real.

"Tom, is it really you?" she stammered like a schoolgirl.

A look of frustration washed over his face. "Do you doubt your own eyes?" he asked.

"Should I? I want for it, for you, to be real but I'm not a child. I know it can't be." What she was saying hurt her almost as much as the wind slapping her face.

He turned away from her, lifted his arm and gestured to a desolate spot behind him in the distance. Paula strained to see what he was pointing at. She saw a small object jutting out of the ground but could not discern exactly what it was. Tom raised both arms and approached the wall. Bringing his hands closer together he formed a barrier that shielded the wind from the opening in the wall.

"You must look closely now," he instructed. "You must see through the winds."

She leaned forward and marveling at how he had managed to obstruct the winds with just his hands, focused on the object and at last she was able to see what it was. It was a flower, a single, bright-red flower that resembled a rose.

How could it survive in the wind? She concluded that it could by the same means by which she was talking to her dead fiancé.

"It's a sign...of survival. It shows that there is always hope, that anything can survive if it has faith."

Paula felt an enormous weight lifted from her shoulders. For the first time since the nightmare began she felt hopeful. Tom smiled as he lowered his arms, forcing her to shield her face from the winds again and back away from the hole even though she did not want to.

"I must go now," he lamented. "But I have something for you." He lifted his arm and produced a small red flower similar to the one in the distance behind him. "To remember me by...forever."

Paula reached out and quickly snatched it from him. Her hand bled from the biting wind but she paid it little notice. All that mattered was the flower and what it represented.

His smile embedded itself in her heart long after he had faded away into nothingness. The empty space where he had stood hurt far worse than the wind, which seemed to be increasing yet again. She reluctantly forced the stone back into its spot on the wall, and using what little water they had, mudded it back into place.

Outside the wall, the flower began to swell. Its pedals wilted and turned a sickly, dirty white in color as enormous, pulsating spores jettisoned out from its center, to be carried by its wind to all corners of the globe for germination. All around it writhing tentacles sprouted up and flailed in the gales like insane dancers, as translucent slime coated its entire mass. It was aware and intelligent, and gyrated from side to side in a grotesque mockery of laughter. An image of Thomas Kannery formed at its base and smiled. It had been easy...real easy.

Paula sat back down on her blanket and looked at the girls; they were still sound asleep. Even the chaos of the wind coming into the cave when she removed rock didn't stir them to consciousness; sheer exhaustion controlled their bodies beyond any doubt.   She lifted the flower and inhaled its fragrance. The aroma was strange, almost unrecognizable, but she realized that it had been awhile since she had last smelled a flower. She set it on the ground beside her blanket and lay down. Sleep visited her quickly and transported her to its peaceful realm; a welcome and much-needed diversion from reality.

The flower arched itself upright and its pedals started to wilt as they changed to a sickly, dirty white color. And then it began to swell.

MEMORIES OF INHUMAN NATURE

The memories floated back into Jeff's mind like colorful, detached leaves wafting down to a front lawn on a crisp fall day. Each and every one displayed its own pain, which it seemed to dole out in completely sporadic intervals. All were difficult to bear, although in different ways and for different reasons, but in some strange way seemingly beyond his comprehension, they were necessary, necessary for closure and for understanding.

He focused on his mother's eyes in one memory. Those soft, warm baby blue windows to her beautiful soul that so many times in his life reflected love and compassion as only a mother's eyes could. He could still see those eyes as clearly as if she were standing right in front of him.

It had been nearly ten years since she had passed away, a victim to a small, seemingly harmless lump in her breast. He honestly thought she would beat it though. She had managed to pull through a serious car accident, a miscarriage and the sudden deaths of both of her parents relatively unscathed. He smiled to himself as he recalled how she had joked how life's problems only served to strengthen her resolve. *What doesn't kill you only makes you stronger,* she would always say and Jeff tried hard to adhere to that philosophy as best he could throughout his life.

Another memory that he recalled was of a lost love that he had. Susie Peters was a very beautiful and petite girl who he had known in high school. She had never really cared that much for him though, outside of a few lackluster hellos and occasionally recognizing that he existed. He fondly remembered her strawberry blond hair framing her milky white complexion and accenting her soft and yet piercing eyes. How he had yearned to speak his true feelings into those eyes and caress that silky hair.

But it was not meant to be, or so he reasoned with himself. He did realize he was basically lying to himself but what else was he to do?

More memories pushed their way into his head. One after the other they stung his mind with various degrees of pain and loneliness. The bleak outlook each brought with it etched away incessantly at his peace of mind and thinned the already delicate barrier between sanity and insanity.

He leaned back in the seat and took several deep breaths. The soft hum of the Dodge's motor gently vibrated the car producing an almost hypnotic effect. His wristwatch yielded the time to him; three- fifteen p.m.

Outside, snow had begun to drift down like tiny flecks of white paint, silent and determined to coat the landscape in its beautiful but cold embrace. He was surprised it had not snowed earlier; it could not have been more than twenty degrees outside with colder weather on the way. Perhaps the snow had just been lazy, he mused to himself; unaware of its duty when the temperature dipped below 32 degrees.

He raised his worn navy blue coffee mug to his lips and took a deep swallow. It had grown stained throughout the years due to the endless cups of coffee it had held and had become a comfortable reminder of better days. He knew he drank too much caffeine but to a certain extent he did not care. His life had not been kind to him and he in turn felt like reciprocating. Why he harbored such irrational and downright absurd feelings he could not explain, not to anyone and certainly not to himself.

Was it due to all he had endured in his life? Perhaps, but many others had endured much worse. Or it simply could be summed up as an excuse, a reason attempting to cling to legitimacy.

Another memory drifted into his consciousness. It demanded to be recognized due to its frightening proportions and steadfastly refused to be understood or explained.

Jeff let a wry smile escape. It was in stark contrast to the nature of the memory but he just couldn't help himself. There shouldn't be any memories of things like these, he reasoned with himself. There just shouldn't. Imaginative thoughts from a horror or science fiction author perhaps but not from a normal, hard-working, responsible man who had managed to face and overcome many unfortunate times in his life.

    The memory played itself out in his mind. A very pretty and obviously distressed young newscast woman filled the television screen. She reported about confirmed assaults on victims in a grocery store parking lot the previous evening. He could still sense the fear that laced her soft voice and blemished her attractive features. She was apparently accustomed to reporting much more mundane stories.

    He felt truly sorry for her; such sweet innocence hardly deserved to be subjected to the dark side of human nature, or worse…inhuman nature.

    He remembered her words became garbled, almost incoherent, no doubt due to the stress of her situation. A large screen directly behind her came to life with a grainy image from a surveillance camera apparently situated on top of a building. It panned the parking lot from one side to the other.

    At first all seemed normal with scattered customers casually strolling to and from their vehicles pushing shopping carts in front of them. Some had small children latched onto their sides. Jeff vividly recalled a small woman of foreign descent setting her bags down to fish her keys out of her purse. She was still rummaging through her belongings when she became aware of someone…or something, on the far side of her truck. In a flash the assailant was on her, easily overpowering her.

    Jeff swallowed hard as he remembered seeing the poor woman fighting for her life with an enormous shadow. It was twisting its flabby bulk as it swung its mockery of a head from side to side. The memory of flailing tentacles from the thing's head stung his sanity repeatedly, driving him ever closer to losing his grip on reality.

    The woman stood no chance against such a powerful adversary and was sucked bags and all into the thing's loathsome abyss. Expansive wings sprouted from its back and within seconds it shot straight into the night sky, gone from sight but not from memory.

He twisted the wiper blade handle on and watched the damp windshield wiped clean. *Strange,* he thought to himself. *How with a simple gesture the state of something could be completely changed around. One minute one way, the next minute something different.*

The distant tree near the end of the street somehow caught his attention. It was large, perhaps an oak or maple, and the shadows it cast on the snow-covered ground were impossible to ignore. Distorted, thin limbs jutted out from its trunk and stretched in every direction like frantic children attempting to flee from a kidnapper. The overall visage of it spawned yet another memory, which like the previous ones was unpleasant and painful.

Images of being alone in his room as a young boy pouring over the literary giants he adored roamed freely in his head. Derleth, Lovecraft, Clark Ashton Smith, they all transposed their will of words upon his mind. He had passed many midnights wandering helplessly in the nether regions of their minds, subject to their horrific whims and vulnerable to their nightmares. The passages spawned in their imaginations littered his thoughts with frightening landscapes which he further contributed to, although without intent, with his own twisted visions.

Visions of the Great Old Ones blotting out the sun with their malevolent bulk, seeking their prey relentlessly across waste-strewn fields clotted his soul and corrupted his sanity. Terrible thoughts of the perverse deity Shub-Niggurath unleashing her Dark Young upon unsuspecting investigators and the Crawling Chaos Nyarlathotep spreading a plague of confusion and madness across the lands seeped into his mind.

His parents had been too late in realizing their only son's descent into the seemingly harmless realm of horror fiction. They had argued constantly about which educational direction their child was going to travel but never really addressed his creative and imaginative pursuits. Fiction, mainly horror, dominated his impressionable young mind and spurred his thoughts, for better or worse, to new levels. He would have hung posters of Cthulhu,

Azathoth or Daoloth on his bedroom walls if it were not for the fact that his parents would have undoubtedly torn them down in an instant; that in addition to not being able to easily obtain such items.

Outside, the snow had abated considerably, reduced to a gentle dusting barley heavy enough to sustain the white ground cover. But what caught his eye and tightened the already twisted knot in his stomach was what lay beneath the snow.

He focused on a small area off to the side of his car. The snow was gradually melting despite the temperature falling, revealing a viscous, black residue underneath. It was thick in consistency, loosely resembling used motor oil and absolute in its color.

Only it wasn't an ordinary shade of black. It was a deep, unyielding black, many times darker than any color on Earth, and it was exposing itself at a rapid pace, swallowing up all traces of the snow and enveloping everything in its path.

Jeff pushed aside the memories that had been assaulting his mind and watched the surrealistic nightmare unfolding outside of the car. An unconditional sea of the substance coated the ground as far as he could see. Its nature or purpose was as curious as it was frightening and the consequences of its appearance chilled his blood.

His mother stood on the sidewalk. She gazed at him with her soft, baby blue eyes as if trying to convey her dire predicament to him. She looked exactly as she had on the day she had died, frail and weary of life. Jeff remembered how much pain she had been in and was surprised and delighted to see that she did not seem to be in any now, despite her appearance. He wanted to leap out of the car and embrace her but thought better of it. He realized that the thing masquerading as his beloved mother was not human and most likely not friendly. He forced himself to look away.

The irrational feelings of turning his back on his dying mother instantly rushed into his head but he suppressed them successfully, content in the knowledge that it was the right thing to do.

    Susie Peters was briskly making her way through the formless black sludge, staring hard at Jeff with her piercing eyes. Specs of the black matter stained her strawberry blond hair and flawless complexion, marring her soft features into a mockery of beauty. An anxious look smeared her face, not unlike a hyena standing over a freshly-slaughtered gazelle, and it sent further chills down his spine. A sickening thought then entered his mind…*he was the gazelle.*

    He closed his eyes tight, so tightly that they hurt. He concentrated on his memories, trying with all his might to secure pleasant ones.

    Misty images of happier times floated about in his head like plump worms on a fishing line, dangling high above eager eyes. He strained to reach them but failed at every attempt. Less friendly ones clung to his mind, bustling to gain access to his consciousness, each a portal to a cold and possibly hostile environment.

    The death of his old dog Dusty and when he had stumbled upon her rigid corpse in the kitchen. The doctor's words informing him that his two lower discs in his back were completely gone and that major surgery was his only option. The disbelief he felt as he watched the tip of his bloody finger drift down into the dust due to his carelessness with the Brush Hog he had been using. All these memories and more clogged his mind and toyed with his strength. He had endured much sorrow and hardship in his life and they had sensed that in him. Perhaps that is what had attracted them to him in the first place. He was a portal, a link to another dimension, to another time in space where unimaginable things squirmed in eager anticipation to advance their malevolent plans.

    The tree stretched out its sizeable limbs and efficiently swatted the mockeries of Jeff's mother and Susie Peters aside. Lumbering its huge bulk down the sidewalk, it crushed all objects in its way as it swung its ropy black tentacles from side to side.

The car was predictably unresponsive to his attempts to shift it into gear and soon stalled out completely. He fondled the small caliber handgun on the seat next to him, debating on whether to use it on the inhuman horrors outside the car or on himself.

Dark Young he recalled they were named, evil servants of the Outer God Shub- Niggurath and spreaders of its faith. The smell of open graves permeated the interior of the car as the tree thing drew nearer. He instinctively rolled the window down and fired five quick shots at the thing, being sure to leave one bullet for himself. Although the attack had no affect whatsoever on the thing it did offer a small amount of satisfaction nonetheless.

He slumped back into the seat and concentrated on happier times. Times when the sun bathed the landscape down with its warmth, times when flowers bloomed and wafted their natural fragrance into the air, times when there were other people still alive. But the memories would not come easily, for more recent and considerably more frightening ones overwhelmed them.

Images of gigantic beings lumbering across waste strewn fields, destroying all in their path played themselves out in his head. Innocent people being scooped up and devoured by forces and intellect beyond their comprehension. Entire cities being ravaged and plundered until nothing remained but charred and lifeless shells littered with smoking corpses and the stench of death.

Jeff reached for the radio in a vain attempt to soften what he had already accepted as his final moments. He knew very well that nothing would come in but he twisted the knob several times nevertheless; pure, irritating static filled his ears. He suppressed the feeling that he was somehow lucky. He was after all quite possibility the last human left alive on the planet. They had undoubtedly kept him around until they were finished with everyone else thus allowing him extra time, which is more than anyone else had gotten.

He slowly opened his eyes and turned his head just as the tree-thing slung its huge limbs around the car. And this time he knew no memories would be able to save him.

WHAT TANGLED WEBS WE WEAVE

Crystal-clear icicles dangled in random lines from nearly every object in the backyard. The wind had picked up slightly, bringing with it a chill, further adding to the gloomy wintery scene as thin plumes of mist rose steadily from the frozen ground. The landscape as a whole had an almost otherworldly aspect to it.

Sierra took a sip of her water as she gazed out through the doorwall glass into the backyard. She could see a little bit of her reflection in that glass, a portrait of a lost woman intent on survival. Tears welled up in her swollen, bloodshot eyes.

If only it could be that simple, she thought to herself. *If only.*

Pangs of hunger incessantly tapped into her mind, searching for any vulnerability in which to break her grip on life. It had been many hours since she had last eaten, too many for any person hoping to stay alive much longer.

A small box of natural grain brown rice stared at her from its perch near the kitchen sink. The thought of tearing it open and devouring it roamed across her mind, but she suppressed the idea. Even in her weakened state she possessed the intelligence to know better. She had to pace herself. She must resist the urges that starvation was placing on her. She must be strong. Only another 30 minutes and then she could eat. She knew she must stick to her rationing schedule; her life could very well depend on it. Eventually someone would come and rescue her.

Eventually? Sounded like a good title for one of her novels. A tortured smile slid across her face, a smile that was well aware of her situation but refused to be restrained nonetheless.

The box of rice was still beckoning to her with its promise of lifesaving nourishment. It stood alone on the countertop flanked by dusty utensils and empty containers of soda pop and juice. The effect it was beginning to have on her psyche was unsettling to say the least. In a sense, it controlled her, entranced her with its suggestions of sustenance.

The sharp scratching sounds from the basement jarred Sierra from her thoughts. They were louder and more pronounced than the previous ones, causing her heart to skip a beat and her empty stomach to convulse.

Was it still in the basement?

The thought that it was fastened itself to her imagination and festered there, attempting to spawn new nightmares.

Of course it was still in the basement. It had to be. There's no way it could have gotten out. But don't you remember the last time you tried to escape? Don't you recall how it was right in front of you in a split second, barring your route to safety? Don't you remember how it SEEMED to still be in the basement when you tiptoed toward the front door? It allowed you a false sense of security, only to rip it out from under you.

The unpleasant memories flooded into her mind suppressing her bravery with their validity. But her time was limited, this she knew all too well. The thing in the basement had cut the phone lines and there was only so much food and water in the house, not to mention only so much air as well. The water and gas had already been shut off and she knew the electricity was next, although she'd probably freeze or starve to death before then. And the fact that she really didn't have any family or friends to check in on her further sapped her hope. All in all, a rather bleak outlook.

And then the noises from the basement stopped suddenly, giving her much needed relief. Apparently the thing in the basement had grown weary of smacking against the door.

Was it doing it simply to frighten her? A ploy intent on loosening her already fragile grip on sanity. Or had it merely grown tired?

Sierra couldn't answer these questions. She decided to try to escape again.

Pushing herself up and out of her chair was difficult but she managed to do it. An eight-inch butcher knife provided security and some old chocolate candies she was saving gave her a little boost of energy.

It's now or never. Not enough food or water to wait any longer. Can't afford to wait any longer.

She thought about trying the doorwall again, or perhaps one of the windows, but she knew they wouldn't open. They never did. The thing in the basement wanted her to go to the front door; it was the only option it offered to her.

Gripping the knife tightly in her hand, she made her way down the dimly-lit hallway. The door to the basement was just around the corner, about ten feet away. There was absolutely no way to avoid it if she wanted to reach the front door; she had to walk past it.

The thing in the basement was making noise again, scratching and whimpering in a pathetic display of distress. But she knew better than to fall for its acting. Once before she had actually believed it was in pain and opened the basement door. In some bizarre way she had felt sorry for it, thinking that maybe, just maybe, all it wanted was to be set free.

Bad decision.

The thing's claws had nearly taken out her throat and succeeded in damaging her already fragile psyche.

She turned the corner and focused on the front door. It stood about 20 feet in front of her, the epitome of the cliché, *so close and yet so far*. On her immediate left was the door to the basement, which was being subjected to various scratching and pushing. It knew she was there and it wanted to get out. She stared at the door in an awkward attempt to diffuse its power, to unravel its mysteries.

"How could this have happened," she screamed. "Why are you doing this to me?"

There was no reply, only frenzied scratching and sporadic growls.

She stood there in the hallway, frozen to the floor, unable to summon enough courage or strength to make a move for the front door. Perhaps she would merely wait for it this time. Allow it to appear and attack it as best she could. One way or the other something would have to give.

After a few moments the sounds from behind the basement door began to subside.

Was it tired? It didn't matter though, now was the time for her to make her move.

She sprinted for the front door. The fact that the knife would have no effect on the thing entered her mind but was quickly pushed aside. All that mattered now was getting out of the house.

The doorknob was in her hand when the chilling sound froze her in her tracks. It was the sound of the basement door creaking open. Attempting to turn the doorknob proved futile so she slowly turned to face her tormentor.

For a second she thought she was looking into a mirror.

The other Sierra stared at her. It made no attempt to communicate or attack; only periodically tilting its head slightly as if pondering its next move. Sickening cracking noises echoed in the room.

Sierra felt her rage boil over. Her weakened condition wouldn't allow her to physically confront the imposter, so she opted for the only alternative.

"What are you?" she asked through gritted teeth.

The other Sierra put a finger to its mouth. As if it were a mother consoling her frightened child she whispered, "Shhhh."

The absurdity of the reply caught Sierra off guard and she found her fear being replaced by confusion. "What are you saying?" she demanded. "What is it you want?"

An oily smile slid across the clone's face. It reached up, and fastening its fingers in its hair, began peeling away the flesh from its face as if it were a zipper. Beneath the skin were glistening scales covered with throbbing pustules, They excreted thick, black ooze. Two boils slithered to the front of the face and fastened themselves where there had previously been eyes. Slits then parted to reveal a new set of eyes, full of hatred and envy.

Sierra screamed and fumbled for the doorknob again but it still wouldn't turn. She threw the knife at the creature but it only bounced off of it and fell to the floor, a useless weapon. She beat her arms on the front window but the glass remained intact. She was trapped.

The thing was advancing on her, slow and deliberately as if trying to extract as much fear from her as it could. The floorboards beneath it feet splintered as it walked on them, leaving in its wake horrible, deformed footprints. Sinewy tentacles sprouted from its sides and began thrashing back and forth like venomous snakes striking out at a potential threat. It wanted her and wasn't going to settle for anything else. It plodded toward its intended victim, all the while gazing at her, bloody slime dripping from its entire body. The hunger it endured was a strong incentive to secure its prey. Its moans filled the room with the despair of its suffering.

And then it was gone.

Sierra turned the doorknob and swung the front door open. She took a deep breath of the warm, spring air, letting it clear her senses and soothe her mind. Behind her, the damaged walls and floorboards were rapidly repairing themselves as the stains from the creature evaporated into the air.

She nudged the basement door closed as she sauntered back into the kitchen. A wry smile formed on her face. The hunger, the thirst, everything right down to the disconnected phone, were all effective tools for her professional occupation. She needed to rely on them constantly to produce the quality product her readers demanded. A good author needs to live the story, to experience all the joy and love…all of the pain and suffering, the characters experience. Only then would the writer truly connect with the reader.

She took a sip of her lemon-ginseng tea and gazed into her backyard, noting that her flowers were starting to bloom. The next chapter in her novel was already forming in her mind, a lengthy one that the story pivoted on. She would try to finish the rough draft by the following month but knew that she couldn't promise her publisher that, not when she was still unsure of the ending.

    And then the sharp, scratching sounds from the basement jarred her from her thoughts.

A NIGHTMARE YOU DON'T WANT TO TEMPT

The swirling collage of disgusting colors flowed relentlessly from one side of the room to the other. Each hue meshed with the ones beside it, creating an entirely new spectrum of shades. The many inanimate objects in the room liquefied as if struggling in a completely alien way to attain life. Chairs jostled back and forth, the television set writhed savagely on its stand, the refrigerator flung its doors open and shut as it moaned and snarled in rage. Even the carpet, a tattered and frayed shag, melted into a filthy pond of nauseating transparency, in which bobbed innumerable, glistening lumps crudely resembling peering eyeballs.

Garrett hated this part of the trip. It usually started toward the end of the buzz but he noticed that lately it had been progressing to the earlier stages. It didn't bother him though, most things didn't. Over the lazy course of his 22 years he had developed, as he liked to refer to it, a hard outer shell that protected him from the troubles and worries of daily life. However, his shell needed nourishment that most effectively came in the form of mind-altering drugs.

His contact, Doug, was a repulsive character, utterly void of the virtues that graced even the lowliest criminals or street bums. But the one thing that Garrett needed him for he always came through with…hooking him up with a fix.

Garrett looked down into his lap at the gleaming syringe. It dripped a bright green liquid from its tip onto his leg. In its cylindrical reservoir were the traces of the drug. He rarely completely finished an injection finding all the protection, as he dubbed it, in about half a dose.

The closet door on the far side of the room swelled as if it were breathing. Its color changed from eggshell white to a bizarre hybrid of angry mauve and washed-out brown. The hinges were straining mightily to contain the door, or whatever lurked behind it, but were clearly losing the battle, filling the room with ear-splitting creaks and clinks.

Garrett shook his head from side to side as if it would help clear it. The inhuman sounds leaking through the door were obvious in their intent and seemed to grow angrier when the human sitting on the couch did nothing. Apparently it did not appreciate its victims merely sitting idly by waiting for their destruction. It preferred prey that had spirit.

Garrett sighed as he began to feel the soft, comfortable clutches of sleep begin to invade his body and mind. The door was nearing its breaking point, which made embracing slumber all the more difficult, but it was overtaking him nonetheless; it was an inevitable and welcome stage of his trip.

He lifted his feet up off of the carpet and marveled at how they were completely dry. Swollen lumps swam in every direction around the couch, occasionally dipping down deep into the carpet on mindless and incomprehensible journeys. The surrealistic vision of this did not deter the peaceful approach of sleep however, and Garrett was starting to pass out as he had so many times before. He was content in the knowledge that he would awaken sometime later in the comfort of his apartment oblivious to the strange carnage and absurd impossibility of what the drug had unleashed upon his senses.

The closet door had switched to a color of red so deep that it bordered on black. The hinges crumbled and plopped into the fetid carpet pond with a sickening thud as the walls around the door split in every direction like blind spiders weaving an insane tapestry of webs.

And then the door collapsed.

Garrett was only partially conscience as the thing menacingly slid into the room. It was ravenous, although confined to a drug-induced nether-region as it had always been it had never really known the joys of eating, but it was anxious to learn.

Its slime-coated cloven hooves trudged through the carpet pond leaving an oily residue in its wake. Garrett glanced at it, and sickened by its visage, quickly looked away, eagerly awaiting the escape sleep so reliably offered.

He passed out just as the thing reached out for him.

The sunlight flooded the room, revealing thousands of otherwise invisible dust particles. Garrett winced as the rays assaulted his face. His head ached and his stomach grumbled in protest to its emptiness as he rubbed his eyes to clear his thoughts. The trip he'd returned from was frightening to say the least but strangely satisfying as well. He'd escaped the troubles of reality successfully and although he now had to face them again he felt refreshed enough to do so adequately. He stood up shakily and stumbled into the kitchen. A hot cup of lemon-ginseng tea is what he needed, that and perhaps a sandwich.

The teapot whistle rang through the apartment, signaling the water within it had reached its boiling point. He removed the lid and tipped the bubbling water into a large coffee mug with a faded half naked woman on it; a 21st birthday gift from his buddies. His head was screaming at him, threatening to unleash a migraine as if in retaliation for the abuse it had endured.

The tea soothed his throat and relaxed his mind. He made a mental note to contact Doug to order a couple more fixes as he started to make a ham sandwich. And then a disturbing fact settled over his good mood…the syringe was missing.

He rushed over to the couch leaving his sandwich on the counter. A frantic and bewildered search revealed no needle or any clues to its whereabouts. He was certain it was in his lap when he tripped out and was sure he hadn't moved it when he woke up. So where was it?

The knob on the closet door creaked as it turned. It violently swung open and slammed into the wall behind it, splintering the drywall and creating a small cloud of dust.

Garrett's heart was in his throat. The darkness inside the closet was perfectly framed by the doorjamb; a clean, black rectangle of the unknown…and all that it contained.

His migraine was stabbing at his head, further complicating the perilous situation he suddenly found himself in.

He was never very good at dealing with life's troubles and now he was going to have to face a big one head on.

The thing entered the room and fixed its loathsome gaze directly on Garrett. It was mostly transparent, giving it an appearance not unlike a distorted ghost. Great pain was etched across its face as every movement it made was accompanied by groans of discomfort. It seemed to be struggling to maintain its solidity in some way.

Garrett was froze to the spot where he stood. He wet himself when it began to stagger toward him, its determination to reach its prey clearly evident on its face.

But that wasn't the worst of it. In its hand it held the key to its freedom and its meal:

Garrett's syringe, which was still dripping a bright green liquid.

THINGS HAVE A WAY OF COMING BACK AROUND

The first sign Randy had that something wasn't quite right was when he left the airport and walked over to the car rental store. Across the street from the store was a florist shop that had several large displays in its front window.

One in particular caught Randy's attention. It was a beautiful collection of white lilies, rimmed with soft pink trim and wrapped loosely in red and white ribbon. And all displayed in an enormous hand-weaved golden basket.

Normally it wouldn't have merited a second glance from Randy, who really didn't care much for flowers, but this particular piece did catch his attention for two reasons.

One: he somehow recognized it, as if he had seen it in a dream.

And two: The inscription on the oversized card nestled in the flowers read:

WITH DEEPEST SYMPATHY FOR MR. RANDY TAILLO. FINALLY AT PEACE.

At first, Randy thought he was imagining things, but after he rubbed his eyes and looked at the card more closely, he knew he wasn't hallucinating.

He thought about going into the store and asking about the strange and coincidental inscription on the card, but something deep down inside stopped him. He somehow knew why the flowers seemed familiar and why his name was on them.

Without waiting another minute, Randy made his way to the car rental store and picked up a newer model Malibu. He didn't really care what type of car it was. All it had to do was get him from point A to point B; A being where he was, and B being his friend Sam's house on the other side of town.

Randy had to get into hiding quickly. He'd managed to pull off his scheme of faking his own death and the last thing he wanted was anyone snooping around asking about his whereabouts.

Guilt lurked around every corner, in every dark recess of his mind. He often wondered if he would be able to live with himself, but reasoned that it wasn't much different than filing for bankruptcy. It was merely another way to start over.

And he'd managed to do it.

The phony funeral was surprisingly easy to pull off. All he had to do was deposit a few stacks of cold, hard cash into the right hands and call in a few favors, and bingo, he was dead. His ex-wife lived in Florida; she moved there after their divorce to start her own new life, and he didn't have any children.

Sam's condo was right out of a movie. It was nearly 5000 square feet and was an unusual design, which allowed it to literally blend into the surrounding countryside. It was supported underneath by a dozen thick pillars of polished pink granite, and cumulated into a towering spiral, which matched the surrounding trees and foliage perfectly.

When Sam answered the door he saw Randy standing on his spacious front porch, panting and quite nervous.

"Randy, you look like you've seen a ghost," he cracked while sipping scotch from an oversized glass.

Randy rolled his eyes at his friend and nudged his way into the house.

"Look Sam," he started. "I really appreciate you letting me stay with you and all, but I gotta tell ya, I've seen some really strange crap ever since I got off the plane."

"Did the stuff I got for you work?" Sam asked calmly, closing the door behind them. He then immediately went and seated himself at his custom-made mahogany bar, pouring himself another drink, as well as one for Randy.

Randy was shaking, causing the ice cubes in his drink to rattle against the glass.

"Yeah, or at least I thought so. Actually I...I don't know."

"Easy there buddy or it will be both our butts. I helped you out because we go way back and you saved my life once. Now you can help me out by not screwing things up. Use the opportunity to make a fresh start with your life. The paperwork is in the works right now. By the end of the week you'll be a new man... literally. You won't have to worry about the people you owe money to. You won't have to worry about your ex-wife. Everybody bought it, I made sure of it."

Randy looked over at his friend, his face marred by worry. "That's if I survive," he lamented.

Sam set his glass down on the bar and walked over to Randy. He was much bigger than his old friend and when he gripped Randy's shoulders he easily forced him to sit down. "Well then, tell me what you saw."

"First, when I left the airport, there was this flower shop. I saw an arrangement in the front window, and they had my freaking name on them! My name! And not only that, I recognized them somehow."

Sam was beginning to doubt his friend's sanity, but played along.

"Go on, tell me what else you saw."

"And then driving down here, off the highway..." Randy paused a moment, trying to find the right words.

"Well?" Sam asked, growing a little impatient.

Sam rolled his eyes and sighed. "What do you mean you didn't see anything?"

"I smelled something."

"You're kidding me, right?"

Randy took a deep breath and began to rub his head. "I know, I know," he continued. "I know it sounds crazy, but I'm telling the truth.

"Okay, take it easy now," Sam consoled. "What did you smell then?" He was beginning to feel like a father humoring his over-imaginative son.

Randy's face hardened like it was made of stone. "I smelled a funeral parlor."

The absurdity of the words struck Sam so hard he had to restrain himself from laughing out loud.

"A funeral parlor?"

"Haven't you ever noticed the aroma at a funeral? The obvious attempts the parlor makes at covering up the natural process of decay."

Sam was at a loss for words. He merely stared at Randy, waiting for what he would say next.

"At a funeral you can smell all the chemicals used on the body. You can smell the casket, the other people there, the flowers." Randy stopped for a moment to make sure Sam was still following him. "That smell, that aroma, that perfumed stench is what I smelled in the car on the way up here." He waited for Sam's reaction. "I know it sounds crazy, but I'm telling you I smelled it. There was no doubt about it. If I closed my eyes I could have sworn I was at an actual funeral."

Sam sat down next to his friend. He was regretting helping him out, but one of his strong beliefs in life was never turn your back on family or friends.

"Randy, now listen to me. You're sounding like you need a straightjacket. I think you need to…"

"You don't think I know what I sound like?" Randy interjected. "But that's not the worst of it."

"Well what is then?"

"When I pulled into your driveway I saw a casket in the bushes."

Sam stood back up abruptly. "You're losing it buddy," he warned. "You really are."

"It wasn't just any coffin. It was the one in my own funeral. I recognized it. It was polished maple with stainless steel and brass hardware. It was the same freakin coffin I crawled into right after I took the drug."

Sam lost it. He'd heard enough. "There's no coffin in my front yard!" he shouted. "Did you use the right dosage like I told you to?"

"Sam, I used the precise amount, just like you said."

"Show me where you saw this coffin then."

The two men walked over to the front door and Randy motioned toward a row of sharply-trimmed yews lining the side of the driveway. His eyes widened in disbelief.

"It…it was right there. I swear it was. I saw it!"

Sam was just about to turn around and refresh his drink when he remembered a rather disturbing fact. The drug Randy had taken was a powerful tranquilizer, which with only a minor amount of tampering could easily induce death-like symptoms that would fool even the most knowledgeable and accomplished of physicians. The man he acquired the drug from was a strange guy named Bantham, who was seriously into the occult. Bantham mixed the drug to the correct proportions and gave it, along with a stern warning, to Sam, who in turn gave it to Randy. The warning was about being careful not to spill any of the mixture, especially on anything inanimate. At the time Sam dismissed the words of caution as nothing more than the rantings of an unstable person. But why the warning about inanimate objects?

Sam was starting to put the pieces together, and Bantham's words were beginning to make sense. He turned to Randy who was still standing next to him, babbling on and on about the coffin he said he saw. Looking him straight in the eye he asked a simple question.

"Randy. Did you spill any of the drug?"

Randy hesitated for a moment before replying.

"I don't think so. I followed your directions and mixed the powder with warm water right before I drank it. Then I finished getting dressed and climbed into the coffin."

"Where?"

"Right there in the back room of the funeral home. Why?"

Sam remembered something else Bantham had said to him, something about the consequences of messing with drugs and altering what's real and what isn't.

"Wait a minute," Randy suddenly interjected. "Come to think of it, when I was about to drink the stuff I think I might have gotten a little bit of it on my hand."

Sam's expression sank to a pale frown.

"I wiped it off on a towel and tossed it on the floor. A man, I think his name was Essel something or other."

Sam's eyes widened. "That's right," he added. "Josh Esslen. He was my contact."

Randy nodded. "Yeah, he helped me finish getting dressed because I was already feeling disoriented. Before I passed out I noticed that Esslen had tossed the towel I'd used onto the coffin lid. The last thing I remember was being wheeled out of the back room and the lid of the casket closing."

Sam walked back to the bar where he quickly finished his drink and promptly poured himself another one. "Randy," he mumbled. "I think you…we have a problem."

Randy continued staring out the front door.

"The guy who mixed the drug for me, he said something about not spilling any of it. This guy was a real weirdo, but he knew his stuff. He said something about respecting everything in life, that everything is bound together with a force, even inanimate objects. In short, everything has a soul."

Randy dropped his drink, the glass shattering on impact.

Sam hardly noticed it though. "And I'll tell you something buddy," he continued. "I think that just maybe some of that stuff was spilled in that funeral home."

"And?"

"And energized the soul in it somehow."

Randy looked down to the floor, his face reflecting his realization of what was happening.

The towel," he muttered under his breath. "The towel."

Sam nodded.

"But as far as I know, it only touched the casket. What about the flowers and that smell in the car?"

"I'm not sure," Sam replied. "All I can think of is…" The revelation struck him at that instant. "Of course," he reasoned. "Why didn't I think of it before? In some parts of the world they consider the funeral rites to be an extension of the deceased, a type of living entity in itself. If some of that stuff was spilled on anything in that funeral parlor it might have…"

"Angered the spirit of the funeral rites," Randy finished.

Suddenly Sam didn't think his friend was crazy anymore. "But I don't think that alone would have been enough. Maybe the fact that you were faking your own death is what did it. What's that smell?"

Randy recognized it instantly. It was the same aroma he had smelled in the car. He turned back around and looked out the front door again. "Formaldehyde," he moaned. "Just like at the funeral. It'll be coming for me. The funeral will be coming for me."

Sam didn't know what to do. His sharp mind raced with options, but he knew deep down inside that the spirits would want anyone associated with the scheme.

The noise coming from the kitchen quickly progressed in both volume and intensity. It sounded as if someone were dragging something heavy across the floor, scraping the ceramic tile as it went.

But Sam knew very well there was nobody else in the house.

"Do you hear that?" Randy asked while frantically looking around for something to use as a weapon.

"Yeah, I heard it," Sam answered quietly. He thought of the gun he kept in his bedroom closet, but knew it wouldn't be of any use. Bullets only work on living things.

Sam watched Randy's eyes expand in fear. He was looking at something, something too terrible to comprehend, something that should not be, but was.

And it was right behind Sam.

Judging from the scraping sounds Sam guessed it was whatever had been in the kitchen. Summoning what courage he had left he whirled around just as the polished maple casket smashed into him.

CHRISTMAS MORNING

Jeremy rolled over in bed and glanced at the clock on his nightstand. *5:55* stared back at him in red LED numbers. A tiny, red dot was lit next to the a.m. designation.

Not even six o'clock yet, he thought sluggishly. *Still too early to get up.*

But the anticipation that he harbored for Christmas morning was severely tempered by the memory of what he had witnessed earlier that same night.

Or thought he had witnessed.

It was shortly after two- thirty a.m. when he woke up, as most children do, overwhelmed by the curiosity of what was under the Christmas tree. With excitement that could only be fostered in a child on that most anticipated of nights, he gleefully crawled out of bed and tip-toed down the stairs to investigate whether or not jolly old Saint Nick had fulfilled his holiday duties.

The Christmas tree illuminated the room in red, green and blue. Jeremy's father didn't like leaving lights on at night, but made an exception on Christmas Eve. Making his way through the room Jeremy kept his eyes on his destination…the Christmas tree, or more accurately, the presents underneath it. He was fearful of breaking his parent's rule about not looking at them before morning, but his curiosity got the better of him.

He paused briefly, taking in the beautiful sight of the room before locking his groggy eyes on the Christmas tree that loomed directly in front of him in the far corner of the room. It stood there, silently guarding the brightly-wrapped treasures beneath it, daring anyone to unwrap them before the morning. It was large, nearly eight feet tall, and was packed with such an assortment of ornaments and tinsel that nearly no green was visible on it at all.

Since Jeremy was an only child he knew that virtually all of the gifts were for him, a thought that increased his excitement ten-fold. It was one of the many perks of not having any brothers or sisters.

Jeremy's heart raced in his chest as he approached the neatly-stacked gifts under the tree. He immediately focused on two of the larger ones, wrapped in bright red and blue wrapping paper respectively, and slid closer to them for a better look. As he reached for the larger one he noticed something out of the corner of his eye.

Something on the tree shifted.

Jeremy looked up from his gifts and watched for any more movement. After a few tense minutes he was satisfied he had imagined it and continued examining his future prizes.

But a small part of his mind wouldn't let go of the movement. It tried to rationalize it but failed to attach any plausible explanation.

A mouse in the tree? A loose branch? A faulty light strand? Possibly, but unlikely.

Jeremy looked at the tree again. It was beautiful, fully lit with shimmering ornaments and dazzling tinsel, but there was something else as well. Something he couldn't explain, but felt nonetheless.

The angel fastened to the top of the tree gazed solemnly across the room. Her flowing garb of gold and blue obscured most of her body, trailing down to mingle with the other decorations. She was the crowning glory of the tree, standing guard year after year from her lofty holiday perch.

Jeremy looked up at her, momentarily forgetting about the presents. He recognized the look in her tiny glass eyes. Even though they weren't real they still conveyed the Christmas spirit. But they also seemed different somehow, more detached from Christmas and less concerned with holiday cheer.

Jeremy's gaze fell upon the presents again. He huddled up close to them, periodically inspecting each and every one as he glanced back at the stairway.

And then he noticed it again.

There was movement in the tree. Only this time it was more pronounced, and in a different area, closer to the top.

Now he was getting nervous. He still wasn't sure if he were imagining it or not, but the uneasy feeling that was settling over the room was unmistakable. He scooted away from the presents and stood up, all the while never taking his eyes off the tree. Slowly turning around his only thought was getting back to the safety of his bedroom. In the morning with the added security of his parents and daylight he could truly enjoy the holiday and tear into his presents.

He resisted the urge to look back as he scurried toward the stairs. He was afraid that he might see something he would regret seeing, possibly for the rest of his life. Within 30 seconds he was tucked safely under his covers trying desperately to fall back asleep.

Jeremy glanced at the clock on his nightstand.

6:17 a.m. Still too early to get up.

Not that he really wanted to get out of bed. But the thought that eventually his parents would come into his room and make him wake up frightened him. They would no doubt be curious as to why their little boy wasn't awake yet on Christmas morning. He would then be obligated to go downstairs with them and open his presents…the ones under the Christmas tree.

Jeremy looked over at the clock again, somehow hoping that time had moved backward.

6:24 a.m. Still too early.

"Good morning, Big Guy," Jeremy's dad bellowed as he flipped on the light switch. ""Don't you want to see what Santa brought this year?" He was gesturing toward the hallway. His mother was standing behind him, beaming from ear to ear, a red and green coffee mug in her hands. Jeremy smiled as best he could and slowly crawled out of bed. Part of him was excited, but another part was scared to death.

"Come on, Big Guy," his dad continued to urge, no doubt reliving his own childhood through his son. "I think you'll be pleasantly surprised. Santa was generous this year."

Jeremy pulled his slippers on and rubbed his eyes. Maybe he just imagined it all; it was the middle of the night, and he hadn't actually seen anything. Excitement began to overtake his thoughts as he stood up and yawned. His parents then ushered him out of his bedroom.

And downstairs, standing in the far corner of the living room, was the Christmas tree. The red, green, and blue lights on it, supplemented by a hint of daylight streaming through the windows, filled the room with holiday cheer.

The tree outside a nearby window was on its side, mostly covered by freshly fallen snow, its pine needles lying on the frozen ground beneath it. It had been discarded carelessly, tossed aside like yesterday's trash.

The Christmas tree shuddered with anxious excitement when it heard the approaching footsteps in the hallway upstairs. It adjusted the angel at its top slightly, one of its many hunting tactics, and waited.

AS MEAN AS THE NIGHT

"Why don't you and your little lady come on over tonight for some cards?" Tony's neighbor Joel asked.

The question caught Tony off guard. He had just finished mowing his lawn, and all he was thinking about was a shower and delving into a good John Saul book. He stopped at the end of his driveway, his lawnmower still warm from its work.

"Well," he stalled. "I...I'm not sure. I'll have to ask Nora." Tony could feel the tension in the air. "She should be back a little later on."

Joel smirked at him, his forehead creasing with his raised eyebrows. "Okay Tony, if you say so. But promise me you'll ask her as soon as she gets home. Me and Janet have been dying to break in a new set of cards."

Joel had always been a strange fellow whom Tony had only known sporadically, occasionally exchanging a few courteous hellos during yard work. Joel's somewhat nosy personality had always put Tony off, and he usually tried to avoid him whenever possible.

Tony forced a fake smile and nodded. "No problem," he lied. "I'll ask her and get back with you."

Joel smiled back an equally false grin and shuffled back to his house.

Tony watched his neighbor, noting the odd way he walked. His feet never really left the ground, almost as if he had a set of skis on. Without another thought he pushed his mower back into his garage. He had no intention of playing cards with his neighbors that night, or any other night for that matter. They were a strange couple, and even though they were his neighbors, he didn't want anything to do with them.

Tony reached for his rake and trimmers. The storm that raged through town the previous night had snapped several branches on his trees, requiring attention that he regretted having to do. He loved his trees, and any damage to them bothered him considerably. He set up his ladder and started cutting into the damaged limbs.

He was leaning too far over on the ladder when he heard an irritating and persistent voice behind him.

"It's all right there, neighbor," Joel chirped. "I'll hold the ladder for ya." He was perched directly behind Tony, his left foot resting on the bottom rung of the ladder, his right planted firmly on the ground.

Tony didn't know what to say.

"And you can pay me back by you and your little lady coming over tonight for cards. Say about seven o'clock?"

Startled by his neighbor's forwardness, Tony craned his neck and looked back at Joel. Beady little blue eyes were riveted to his, eyes that refused to reveal their true nature.

"Say," Tony remarked. "Didn't you used to have hazel eyes?" he regretted the words as soon as they left his mouth.

Joel's expression darkened. "What's really on your mind, neighbor?"

"N...nothing," Tony stammered. "I just thought your eyes were..."

"Contacts," Joel quickly corrected. "They're easier than glasses."

Tony nodded suspiciously. "Sure," he agreed with a shaky grin. "I guess so."

"Anyway, seven o'clock sharp. And don't be late."

"But I didn't..."

"See you then, neighbor."

Tony watched Joel shuffle back to his house in the same weird manner he had before, his feet never really leaving the ground, sliding across the grass in short, quick movements.

Nora pulled into the driveway at that moment and Tony practically leaped off the ladder and ran to her car.

"Honey," he panted. "Joel next door invited us over for cards tonight."

He waited for her reaction, not realizing that he hadn't said anything about the unusual way Joel had acted. When she merely shrugged he quickly added more facts.

He told her about the different color eyes. He told her about the strange way Joel walked. He told her about how Joel seemed to appear out of nowhere by the ladder and practically insisted on cards that night. But nothing seemed to faze her.

"Tony," she stated in a dull, indulgent tone. "Why don't we go over and play some cards with them tonight? After all, they are our neighbors."

"But his eyes!"

"Didn't you ask him about them?"

"Well, yeah. He said they were contacts."

"So what's the problem then? It's all in your imagination."

Tony was frustrated, but also relieved. Maybe he was just being paranoid. And perhaps some cards would be fun, get his mind off things a little. He decided then and there that he would give Joel the benefit of the doubt.

*   *   *   *

The movement was slight, almost unnoticeable, but it was there nonetheless. A slender appendage of some sort squirmed in the grass…

Joel's grass.

It was small, about the size of a broom handle, and undulated like a snake, its pale blue color strangely reflecting the sunlight.

Tony stood perfectly still, transfixed by it, unable to take his eyes off of it. His mind attempted to fasten a logical conclusion to the thing, but struggled to accept any notions he came up with.

And then the thing seemed to sense him watching it. It wriggled up and down a few times and quickly vanished into the grass, leaving no trace behind except for a few thin depressions in the lawn.

Tony immediately rushed over to Joel's yard and frantically scanned the ground for the creature. His heart beat wildly in his chest, threatening to stop at any moment, but he carried on, intent on proving to himself that he wasn't imagining what he saw.

"Looking for something?"

Tony's blood froze in his veins. Joel was standing behind him, a thin smile plastered across his face.

"I...I was just..."

"It's all right, neighbor," Joel interrupted. "See you tonight." And with that he shuffled back into his house.

Tony watched him leave, again noting how his feet never appeared to leave the ground. And he also thought of another disturbing fact:

Joel's eyes were hazel again.

Tony wanted to run into his house and tell Nora about what he saw, but thought better of it. No doubt she'd think he was imagining things again. Instead, he opted for a more subtle approach. He and Nora would go over to Joel's house that night for cards, and he would keep a sharp eye out for anything strange.

*   *   *   *

As seven o'clock neared Tony couldn't deny to himself that he was nervous. He thought he had a grip on it, concluding that he was just being paranoid, but the thought that something might be wrong nagged at his mind incessantly.

The sun was hanging low in the darkening sky, preparing to let night take over. Tony walked out onto his front porch and glanced at his watch. Joel's house stood next to his, a mere 25 feet apart, like two children huddling around a campfire.

"Six fifty-six," he mumbled to himself while fondling his pocketknife in his slacks. The knife was small, but sharp, and he had grown quite adept with it over the years. If there was any trouble he felt comfortable with it in his hand.

He wondered where Nora was, and was about to call out for her when his neighbor's dog caught his attention.

Cookie was a cute little rascal. She was a beagle mix with sandy brown hair and a friendly personality. Tony frequently tossed her half of his morning bagel if no one was watching.

"Hey there Cookie," he called out to the dog. "What ya doing over there, girl?"

The dog lifted its head up out of the grass and fixed its gaze directly on Tony. A dark glint reflected in its eyes, a spark of malevolence normally impossible for a dog to express.

Even from the distance between the two of them Tony sensed something was not quite right about Cookie. He instinctively took a step back toward his front door, partially intent on escaping into the sanctuary of his house if need be.

A low growl drifted from the dog and resonated off the house. Its mouth opened and shut repeatedly, blackened foam dribbling down its chest.

"W…what's the matter girl?" Tony stuttered. His hand slipped into his pocket and cradled his pocketknife.

Cookie continued to glare at him, her snarls becoming more labored, deeper, more pronounced. Her fur bristled with the wind, flowing wildly around her body.

A chill ran down Tony' spine when he realized that there was no wind whatsoever. The trees stood perfectly still, and his United States flag hung vertically against the flagpole next to his house.

And then he watched in horror as Cookie suddenly flopped to the ground and began shaking violently. His macabre fascination took over, and similar to people watching the aftermaths of car accidents, he stared at his neighbor's dog in its apparent distress.

Cookie was convulsing. Sudden, obviously painful movements racked her body, and her face twisted into something akin to a distorted, animated mockery of a dog. The thin, pale blue tentacles, which were attached to her sides, squirmed and glistened in the sun, coated heavily with a gelatinous substance resembling saliva.

Tony then noticed that the appendages were not burrowing into the poor creature, but were somehow a part of it! They writhed like worms blindly searching for carrion to feed on.

And then, as quickly as she had fallen over, Cookie abruptly stood back up, and throwing a vicious stare at Tony, shuffled back into Joel's house, her sodden paws never leaving the ground.

Tony stood paralyzed. He had just witnessed something impossible, something that couldn't possibly have happened, but did. And it happened right in front of him.

"Are you okay, Honey?" Nora asked as she casually sauntered out onto the porch. "You look like you've seen a ghost."

Tony managed a weak smile. "Maybe we should stay home tonight," he mumbled. He wanted to tell her what he had just seen, but was afraid she would think he was crazy. And what really frightened him was the possibility that she would've have been right.

He decided to feign illness. "I have a bad headache, and my stomach doesn't feel right." He could only hope she would buy his act.

"Are you sure, Honey?" she asked sympathetically. "Although you do look little pale," she noted. "But then again, I really think we should still go, at least for a little while."

"But Nora…"

"There you guys are." It was Joel. He was standing near Tony's front porch, grinning from ear to ear. "I was beginning to wonder if you folks were gonna make it tonight." As he spoke he was gesturing toward his own front door, that was wide open, revealing a thick wall of darkness inside.

Tony eyed him suspiciously, occasionally glancing down at his feet, which were firmly rooted to the ground. "I'm afraid I don't feel that well," he lied. "Maybe another night." He watched Joel for a reaction.

Joel's smile quickly disappeared. "I suppose so," he sighed. "Hope you're feeling better." And then he shambled back into his house.

"That's odd," Nora said from behind him.

"What?"

"How he walks. His feet never seem to leave the ground."

Tony felt relieved, but also frightened. "I saw it too," he added. "And his dog, Cookie..."

"What about his dog?"

"I saw her in Joel's yard. She fell over, and there were these...things attached to her, like snakes."

"Snakes?"

"Well, yeah. Tentacles. I saw it Nora. I..."

Nora's stare cut off Tony in mid-sentence, her stern expression speaking volumes.

Tony quickly tried to defend himself. "I know it sounds crazy, but I'm telling the truth."

"And when exactly did you start noticing these things?" Nora asked sarcastically.

"Come to think of it," Tony answered. "It was right after the big storm came through town last night. Before that everything seemed normal." He glanced over at Joel's house. "Everything seemed normal."

*   *   *   *

For the next few days Tony watched his neighbor's home closely. He studied it, noting how dirt and leaves never seemed to cling to it; it always appeared clean. He noticed that animals avoided it. Birds, squirrels, even insects, no living creatures ever went near it. Nora took notice of her husband's strange obsession with their neighbor's house too, and despite occasional remarks about his paranoia, generally let him be.

"How ya doing, Tony?" It was Joel again. As he had done before, he came up behind Tony as he was climbing into his car to go to work. "We gotta set up another time for you and Nora to come over." His face glowed with excitement.

Tony nudged him aside and quickly got into his car. He slipped the key into the ignition and turned to face the window. Joel's sweaty face was pressed against the glass, his breath fogging up the window.

"Where ya going, buddy?" he asked with a sneer. "What's your hurry?" His eyes were wild and unblinking, resembling a starved lion approaching a pack of gazelles.

Tony didn't know what to do. His initial instinct was to start the car and get away, but Joel was practically glued to the side of the vehicle, hindering Tony's decision-making abilities.

"Get away from my car Joel," he warned. "I have to go to work."

Joel glanced down for a second, and then slid back a few feet. He looked confused, as if he were awaiting instructions on how to proceed.

And then, without warning he lunged for the car, smashing the window and tearing at the door. Tony watched in disbelief as his car door was ripped clean off its hinges and flung high into the air. It landed twenty feet away, crashing to the concrete in a twisted pile of metal.

"Come on now neighbor," Joel snorted. He had the look of a homicidal maniac, only veiled slightly with a mask of friendliness. "Janet and I have the card table all set up. Isn't that right, Honey?"

"Yes dear, that's right." Janet, Joel's shapely wife, was sliding out the back door of her house, a sly grin plastered across her pretty face.

Tony couldn't help but notice that she moved the same odd way Joel did, her feet never leaving the ground, almost as if she were on a conveyer belt. He watched as she came closer and closer, her features growing more distinct, more distorted with each passing second. Without taking his eyes off her, he reached beneath the car seat and whipped out his tire iron. A smile crept across his face when he thought of Nora nagging him to keep it in the trunk. But after the last few days he felt better with it under the seat.

He swung the tool in a sideways slashing motion, striking Joel just below his midsection. A part of him wanted to hold back, just in case it really was his neighbor, but his instinct to survive dictated his actions.

Joel howled in pain. The top portion of his body slid off the lower part, falling to the driveway in a bloody heap of steaming gore. Sinewy, pale blue tentacles sprouted up from the still-standing legs, and promptly scooped up the rest of the body. In a flash, the whole mess retreated back into Joel's house.

The relief Tony felt was short-lived because Janet was coming straight at him, her pink sneakers dangling uselessly from the tentacles that used to be her legs. She was seething with rage.

Leaping from his car Tony sprinted toward the safety of his house. Nora, who was stepping out onto the front porch to see what all the commotion was, was literally pushed back into the house by her husband.

"Tony! What's going on?"

Without bothering to answer her Tony made a mad dash for his shotgun mounted above the fireplace.

"Lock the doors!" he demanded.

Nora stood frozen for a moment, shocked by her husband's behavior, but snapped out of it when she glanced out the front bay window.

Janet was pressed against the glass, pale blue tentacles waving menacingly around her body.

"Don't look at it!" Tony shouted while fumbling with the gun. "It's not Janet! It's not human!"

But Nora couldn't help herself. She was staring at the creature, and also what was behind it:

her other neighbors.

There were dozens of them, running for their lives in all directions. She saw Mr. and Mrs. Tollin, an elderly couple who recently celebrated their 60th wedding anniversary. She noticed Johnny Fredricks, who raced cars on the weekends, and was still in his grease-stained overalls. She watched Helen Challinty, a single twenty-something medical student. She saw all of them and many others, people she'd seen almost every day going about their business, leaving for work, cutting their grass. And now they were trying to escape from masses of tentacles slithering across the street, over front lawns, and into homes. Tentacles that originated from Joel and Janet's house.

The destructive appendages twisted and turned in every direction, and with frightening speed and agility. They smashed everything in their path in their seemingly blind hunt for prey.

"Tony," Nora said in a calm tone considering the carnage she was witnessing. "There's things outside attacking people."

Tony had finally succeeded in loading the shotgun, and whirled around to face the bay window. He stared at Janet for a second, noting how there still seemed to be a trace of humanity in the expression, but raised his gun regardless. Behind Janet he saw a young boy being dragged to his death by a tentacle the size of a man's leg.

"Tony," Janet cooed in a deceptively pleasant tone. "You killed my husband. But don't worry, I forgive you. Now let me in and we'll talk about it." And then she reared back and smashed headfirst into the glass.

Nora screamed as she shielded her face from the flying onslaught of glass. Tony leveled the shotgun at Janet and then raised it higher, aiming as best he could at Joel's house instead. And then he unloaded both barrels directly into the building.

The house shook violently, shifting back and forth as if trying to dodge the attack. But it was no use. The pellets bore straight into the sides of it, sending chunks of blackened wood and glass crashing to the ground below.

Tony watched dumbfounded as Janet shivered as if someone had rammed a butcher knife into her back. With a choked groan of pain she straightened up and was yanked backward with such force that Tony only saw a blur.

And then an uneasy silence settled on the scene. Still gripping his shotgun in his hands, Tony slowly approached the bay window. The carnage was devastating and all encompassing. Broken bodies were strewn across front lawns; cars were crunched down to unrecognizable lumps of metal; and trees were splintered like matchsticks. And above it all, the sky was darkened by the blood of innocents, stained forevermore from the murderous abomination from another world, another time, another dimension.

Nora walked up behind Tony and took his hand in hers. "Where did it come from?" she asked. Her tone was marred from shock, from the fact that their lives, everyone's lives would never be the same again.

"I honestly don't know," Tony replied through a forced smile. "But I do know that whatever it is, it's dead."

Nora nodded. "But there's something else that worries me," she added. "What if there are more of them?"

Tony swallowed hard. That rather disturbing thought hadn't occurred to him yet. "You mean in other cities? In other neighborhoods?"

The house began to shift at that moment, contorting itself as if trying to shed an outer skin. A deep, throaty groan shook the house then, and a foul smell permeated the room the couple was standing in.

Tony tried to remember just where he'd left the other box of shells. In the panic of the attack he had dropped them, and now they could be anywhere. His blood froze in his veins when he felt Nora's hand begin to change, elongating, becoming moist and cold. He tilted his head down and saw he was holding a sinewy tentacle, a pale blue thing that writhed like an injured worm.

"Other cities?" Nora's unchanged voice whispered. "Other neighborhoods? Perhaps. But I was referring to this one."